S0-EHX-512

A
SPOONFUL
OF TIME

A Spoonful of Time

FLORA AHN

ILLUSTRATIONS BY JENNY PARK

QUIRK BOOKS

PHILADELPHIA

Library of Congress Cataloging-in-Publication Data
Names: Ahn, Flora, author. | Park, Jenny (Illustrator), illustrator.
Title: A spoonful of time / by Flora Ahn; illustrated by Jenny Park.
Description: Philadelphia : Quirk Books, [2023] | Audience: Ages 8-12. | Audience: Grades 4-6. | Summary: "Maya discovers stories and secrets from her family's past in Korea as her grandmother teaches her to cook and about their family's ability to time travel into memories via food"—Provided by publisher.
Identifiers: LCCN 2022031150 (print) | LCCN 2022031151 (ebook) | ISBN 9781683693185 (hardcover) | ISBN 9781683693192 (ebook)
Subjects: CYAC: Time travel—Fiction. | Memory—Fiction. | Food—Fiction. | Families—Fiction. | Secrets—Fiction. | Korean Americans—Fiction. | Korea—Fiction.
Classification: LCC PZ7.1.A3459 Sp 2023 (print) | LCC PZ7.1.A3459 (ebook) | DDC [Fic]—dc23
LC record available at https://lccn.loc.gov/2022031150
LC ebook record available at https://lccn.loc.gov/2022031151

ISBN: 978-1-68369-318-5

Printed in the United States of America

Typeset in Minion Pro

Designed by Andie Reid
Illustrations by Jenny Park
Production management by John J. McGurk

Quirk Books
215 Church Street
Philadelphia, PA 19106
quirkbooks.com

10 9 8 7 6 5 4 3 2 1

To Mom and Dad,
for the many meals we shared
and stories you told

CONTENTS

CHAPTER 1

PATBINGSU WEATHER

"It's patbingsu weather."

Maya almost didn't hear her grandmother over the whir of the fan and the rumbling snores of Gizmo, the old, lazy pug dog squished by her side. Dropping her journal, she rolled over and slowly pulled the backs of her arms and legs off the thin bamboo sticks of the mat beneath her. Her grandmother shuffled past her into the kitchen, a dusty box in her arms.

"Did you ask me something, Halmunee?" Maya asked, hoping the answer was no. It was too hot to even think about moving. After three long days of blazing August heat and no AC, Maya had finally dragged the bamboo mat out of the garage and into the living room. The mat was supposed to keep a person cool, but it could only do so much. It didn't help that no matter where she lay, Gizmo scooted up as close to her as possible, his warm fur pressed against her like a hot-water bottle.

With a soft grunt, Halmunee heaved the box onto the counter, then turned to shout back at Maya. "I said, it's patbingsu weather."

Relieved that Halmunee didn't seem to need her help, Maya flopped back onto the mat and picked up her journal.

Growing up in the cracks of her mother's busy work schedule meant Maya was accustomed to entertaining herself and living in a quiet world. The thoughts and unanswered questions that often raced through her mind found their home in the form of scribbles and drawings in a small journal she usually carried with her. Maya constantly felt the urge to draw. She didn't know where it came from since neither Mom nor Halmunee was capable of drawing even a straight line. She often wondered if she got her love of drawing from her father.

As soon as she filled up all the pages in a journal, she placed it in her bookshelf in a row hidden behind her ordinary books. She had started doing this two years ago on her eleventh birthday, when Mom had given her a blue journal with Maya's name etched in silver at the bottom corner.

Her mom was often tired and distracted in the evenings and on weekends, and some days she could go for several hours without uttering a single word. For as long as Maya could remember, it had been just her and her mom in their still and silent house.

But then Halmunee arrived. And Halmunee didn't live by the same rules.

When Maya craved attention or someone to talk to, she loved having Halmunee there, someone who always wanted to know how her day went and what she had drawn in her journal recently. But during moments like this, when Maya wanted to move and talk as little as possible, a tiny part of her wished for the times before Halmunee came to live with them—for those uneventful days of quiet and calm.

Pat! Bing! Su!

She smiled to herself. Maya could picture those staccato syllables exploding from balloons, or maybe spilling out of a popcorn maker. Drawing her questions was often more fun than learning the actual answers.

Maya returned to her journal, lost in another world as she flipped to a new page to draw the word *patbingsu*.

"It really is the perfect weather for patbingsu," said Halmunee, now standing directly behind Maya. "I think this would be a good time for me to show you something new."

Halmunee had tried a few times before to tempt Maya to cook Korean food with her. Each time, Halmunee got more stubbornly insistent. But Maya didn't have much experience in the kitchen and it seemed like a lot of work, cooking everything from scratch.

When it was clear that Maya wasn't going to volunteer any further interest, Halmunee nudged her and continued. "You'll like it. Come into the kitchen and help me with this."

Maya groaned. The kitchen was the hottest spot in their house!

Halmunee ignored Maya's protest and shuffled back into the kitchen. "Here. Help me lift this out."

Maya got up and readjusted the clothes that had bunched up on her sweaty skin. Small beads of sweat sprouted on her forehead as she entered the kitchen and trudged over to where Halmunee stood.

At her movement, Gizmo quirked his head to the side and wiggled himself up to follow after her. He was the laziest dog in the world and could spend hours sleeping in one spot, but he never missed a potential opportunity for food.

As instructed, Maya held onto the box while Halmunee pulled out a small, white appliance with a wide base and a bulky top.

"I've never seen a patbingsu before," Maya said, using a finger to trace the faded dancing penguins that decorated the appliance. She wasn't impressed. This was definitely not more interesting than her journal drawing.

Halmunee laughed. "No, this isn't patbingsu, silly. This is what we use to make patbingsu. You haven't seen this again yet?"

Maya shook her head.

"This is an ice-making machine." Halmunee frowned. "No, that's not right. It doesn't make ice. It makes the snow."

"The snow," Maya echoed. Her gaze darted nervously across Halmunee's face, looking for any sign of the frustration or anxiety that sometimes overwhelmed her grandmother as she searched for words, phrases, or names that she once knew. When Halmunee had first arrived to live with them several months ago, Mom had briefly told Maya about dementia and how it made a person forgetful. Without any further explanation, Mom had sighed and gone off to bed, leaving Maya confused. It wasn't until the next day that Maya realized Mom had been talking about Halmunee.

Since that day, Maya hadn't had a chance to discuss it further with Mom. Over the past few months, Mom seemed to always be in a bad mood or suffering from a migraine. She was easily irritated, especially if Maya tried bringing up anything related to Halmunee.

"The snow," said Halmunee. "You know. The snow you eat?"

Relief shot through Maya's body as she realized what Halmunee meant. "Oh, you mean like snow cones! Yeah, I've had those before. But not at home."

As Maya squinted at the ice machine, the cartoonish penguins seemed a little more familiar, but she couldn't be certain if that was based on a real memory or wishful thinking.

Had Mom made this same dish for her when she was little? Or maybe this machine belonged to Dad? Was it a memento of his that was too painful for Mom to look at? Maybe that was why she had boxed it up and put it in the garage to be forgotten.

Halmunee wiped the ice machine with a damp towel. "Every summer in Korea we love eating patbingsu. When I was young, and before we had refrigerators and freezers in every house, I would go to my local bakery to get patbingsu. Snow cones are all syrup and sugar. I know what they are. They're just like the too-sweet treats that street vendors would sell from melting blocks of ice they carried in carts. Patbingsu is better. It has red beans and fruit."

Maya made a face. "Beans?"

"Trust me," said Halmunee. "You'll like what I'm going to show you."

Maya bit back any further protest. An icy treat right now would help cool things down. Plus, Mom barely made anything anymore. The most she did these days was make a quick pasta using whatever sauce in a jar had been on sale that week and whatever vegetables Maya could find in the refrigerator. So as much as the thought of beans and ice together repulsed Maya, she was a little curious. Halmunee had finally worn her down, and Maya settled into the position of an assistant with Halmunee as the head chef.

"What can I do?" she asked.

Halmunee smiled at her. "I already have the red beans and rice cakes. So, all we have to do now is cut the fruit and make the snow."

Halmunee put two small bowls in the freezer to chill while they cut a banana, a peeled kiwi, and a few strawberries into bite-sized pieces. Occasionally, Halmunee would bump Maya's hip to get her attention, just like Mom often did.

Maya dropped ice cubes into the top of the machine and Halmunee pressed down to crush the ice. The machine was so loud it drowned out all other sounds and made Gizmo scurry away to lurk just behind the kitchen doorframe.

Then Maya collected the bowls from the freezer. She cradled the icy-cold surface against her warm skin, instantly cooling herself down and sending a shiver down her spine. Halmunee filled the bowls with the homemade snow and spooned in a cold mixture of sweetened red beans. Maya helped to arrange the fruit and rice cakes around the mounds of ice and beans as Halmunee drizzled some condensed milk over them.

"Now comes the best part of cooking," said Halmunee with a grin. "Eating!"

Maya grinned back and dug into the patbingsu, careful to get a bit of each ingredient into her first bite. A shock of cold pinged from her teeth through her core and down to her toes. She let the ice melt down her throat, savoring everything, from the taste of the sweet beans and fruit to the chewy texture of the tiny cube of rice cake. Maya dug her spoon back into the patbingsu for a second, bigger bite. She looked up to see Halmunee watching her eat.

"See?" said Halmunee. "I told you you'd like it. You'll like this part, too."

Before Maya could wonder what she meant, Halmunee reached over and squeezed Maya's hand. The chill of Halmunee's frozen fingers made Maya shiver again. And then, the world ripped away in a blur.

PATBINGSU

By Halmunee, *edited with specific measurements by Maya!*

〜〜〜〜〜

1–2 scoops of shaved ice

Sweet red beans (2–4 tbsp, to taste)

Various fruits (strawberries, blueberries, and/or kiwis, chopped)

Sweetened condensed milk (2 tbsp)

Small rice cake pieces (available at the Korean market)

1. Put a bowl in the freezer to chill.

2. Using an ice machine, blender, or food processor, crunch up the ice to a snow-like texture.

3. Put a couple of scoops of shaved ice in the bottom of a bowl.

4. Pour a few spoonfuls of sweetened red beans on top.

5. Add as much chopped fruit on top as you want!

6. Pour a couple of spoonfuls of sweetened condensed milk over the ice, fruit, and red beans.

7. Add a few small rice cake pieces on top.

8. Patbingsu tastes best on a hot summer day. Eat it quickly before it melts!

CHAPTER 2

NOT A DREAM

A cacophony of sounds, images, and smells flooded Maya's senses so quickly and so completely, she couldn't separate or identify a single one. She could only focus on the pressure of Halmunee's hand holding her own.

Then, like the end of a roller coaster ride, it stopped as suddenly as it started.

Stunned, Maya rooted to the ground and concentrated on trying not to fall or get sick.

Halmunee was gone. Gizmo was gone. The kitchen was gone.

A strong summer sun beat down on her, and cicadas buzzed in her ears. Maya was standing in the middle of a yard filled with leafy plants and neatly trimmed trees laden with dangling persimmons. A small house faced her, its door ajar. She stepped toward it, but a squeal of laughter made her whirl around.

A few feet away, an old weather-beaten table grew out of the tall grass. It was flanked on both sides by matching benches. A handsome man sat on one of them, bouncing a little girl on his knee.

They were playfully fighting over a giant bowl of patbingsu in front of them. Their long-handled silver spoons chimed like music as they dueled over the icy prize softening in the blazing heat.

Maya's own spoonful of patbingsu dribbled down the front of her shirt as she gawked at them. There was something familiar about the man.

Harabujee?

But that was impossible. This couldn't be her grandfather. He'd died long before she was even born. And, even if he were alive, he'd be old. Like Halmunee.

And yet, here he was. Looking not that much older than he did in the only photo of him Maya had ever seen.

A photo that was taken almost fifty years ago.

For Maya, Harabujee really only existed in that single picture from his wedding that sat atop Halmunee's dresser. Halmunee said that she had stumbled across the old photo, with its curled and peeling edges, in a crumpled box in the back of the garage. Maya knew every last detail of it and had carefully copied the image of her young grandparents in her journal over and over again, tracing the features of their faces until they felt as familiar as her own. Now, any time Maya went into Halmunee's room to fetch her for dinner or bring her some tea, she'd pause to study it for a few seconds. The crisp lines of Harabujee's suit. His thick, shiny hair. The faint markings in the corner that said: "Kim Young Soo and Kim Hyun Suk, wedding 1975."

But, unlike in the wedding photo where he stood straight and serious, here Harabujee was in constant motion, laughing and making dramatic swooping gestures with his spoon.

The little girl on his lap squealed and shouted, "Appa!"

Maya blinked.

Appa? The little girl was his daughter?

Harabujee and Halmunee had only one daughter.

Yoo Jin, Maya's mother.

Maya shuffled closer. With each step, she waited for Harabujee and Yoo Jin to look up and notice her. But they never did.

Maya and her mother had always closely resembled each other, but as a girl with long hair and round cheeks, little Mom looked even more like Maya. They both had wide-set eyes, eyebrows that arched in a permanent question, and full lips that formed an almost perfect circle.

Maya couldn't remember the last time she'd seen Mom as happy as this little girl was. She wondered if she herself had been as happy when she was this young.

She doubted it.

Maya had almost forgotten about Halmunee, so when her grandmother appeared seemingly from nowhere and meandered toward the table to run her wrinkled hand through Harabujee's hair, Maya jumped and dropped her spoon.

Halmunee's hand went right through Harabujee. As if she were the ghost from the past, not him.

Halmunee looked at Maya and smiled, a mischievous glint in her eyes.

Maya pinched the inside of her arm and registered the slight twinge of pain. Great. Not a dream.

How could this be happening? Time travel wasn't real. It was something to read about or watch in a movie, to live vicariously through beloved characters, because, again, time travel wasn't real.

Just as Maya felt herself sinking into a deeper level of panic, a shout pierced her thoughts.

"Yah! What are you doing?"

Maya had difficulty speaking Korean, but her comprehension was just fine, and she immediately recognized that those words meant trouble. She instinctively stood straighter and assumed her best "Who, me?" expression.

The door of the house was now wide open and a young woman was leaning against the doorframe. This woman looked so much like Mom that Maya stared at her, confused, for several seconds.

Maya's gaze took in the woman's teased hair that had been smoothed into sleek and bouncy curls, her winged eyeliner, and her short, colorful patterned dress that showed off her trim figure.

No, this wasn't Mom. She had the same face, but everything else about her screamed another era. This was a younger, 1970s mod version of Halmunee.

This was Kim Hyun Suk. Not the white-haired, wrinkled grand-mother Maya knew, but the youthful mother to little Yoo Jin and wife to Kim Young Soo.

Hyun Suk pushed herself away from the doorframe and slipped her feet into a pair of sandals that sat by the door. The dense grass muted the slap of her sandals as she approached her husband and daughter.

"You're supposed to eat this, not play with it and make a sticky mess." The grin on Hyun Suk's face took the edge out of her reprimand, and she lost all claim to stern authority when she stole Young Soo's spoon and scooped up a heaping pile of patbingsu.

Young Soo laughed and shouted to his daughter, "Quick! We must defend the treasure!"

With a delighted shriek and squeal, Yoo Jin licked her spoon clean and jabbed it into the air, challenging her mother to battle. Soon, Yoo Jin had the bowl within the protective circle of her arms and most of the remaining patbingsu either in her stomach or on her face. Hyun Suk and Young Soo smiled at each other over their daughter's head as she slurped up the last melted bits from the bowl.

"Perfect patbingsu weather," Young Soo said, his voice lazy with contentment.

Hyun Suk nodded. "Perfect."

The word echoed through Maya's ears as another voice next to her agreed. "Perfect."

Maya turned as Halmunee sidled up to her and linked their arms.

"See," said Halmunee. "I told you it was perfect weather for patbingsu. Aren't you glad I made you take out the ice machine?"

Maya's gaze flickered back and forth between Halmunee and Hyun Suk. The same faces, a lifetime apart.

"But . . . what is this?" she asked. "Is this real?"

"Of course." Halmunee patted her arm and didn't offer any further explanation. Maybe to Halmunee, nothing about this was wrong. Maybe she was so used to the past knocking on her door and flooding her present, none of this struck her as strange at all.

But this was strange. Very, very strange.

Maya had so many questions buzzing around her head, she didn't know which to ask first. She opened her mouth and they tumbled out, one after another with barely a breath between. "But how is this possible? How can you be here and there? How come they can't see us? Where are we? Wait, *when* are we?"

"Where?" True to form, Halmunee zeroed in on one of Maya's questions and ignored the rest. This was only partially a result of Halmunee's condition. Even on good days, she answered only the questions she felt like answering. It drove Mom crazy, but a stubborn streak ran through their family; both Maya and Mom were just as guilty of doing the same.

Halmunee gestured toward the small house behind them. "We're here. Our house."

Maya closed her eyes. Great. She was stuck in some sort of bizarro world and her only guide was her grandmother, who was so confused she kept mistaking the past for the present.

Halmunee poked Maya in the ribs twice, until Maya opened her eyes and looked at her.

"Wake up," said Halmunee. "What are you doing? It's time."

"Time for *what*?" Maya didn't mean to snap at Halmunee, but her normal world was completely gone, and with it went her usual sense of calm. As much as she liked to read about wild adventures, she never wished for any of them to actually happen. It had been hard enough adjusting to the disruption that Halmunee brought with her when she moved in, and this was beyond any of that. This was beyond reality.

"Time to go home, silly," Halmunee said.

"Home?" Maya echoed. She looked toward the small house and her shoulders sagged. That house wasn't her home. This *time* wasn't even her home.

Trying not to get too bogged down in despair, Maya latched onto a tiny glimmer of hope. Maybe there would be some useful information inside the house that could help her figure out how to get back to the present, she thought. She just had to take this one step at a time and not panic.

Hyun Suk and Young Soo rose from the table and swung their daughter between them as they walked across the yard.

"We were so happy," said Halmunee. "It was all as it should be. Inyeon."

Maya had never heard that word before.

"What's that?" she asked.

"Destiny." Halmunee switched to Korean with her next words. "Even the brushing of sleeves with someone is fate."

Maya didn't know what Halmunee was talking about and didn't know how to respond. But she didn't want to lose sight of her grandparents, so she moved forward to follow them. A surprisingly strong grip on her arm held her back.

"Where are you going?" asked Halmunee.

"To the house." Maya gestured toward the house before them.

Halmunee waved her hand dismissively. "No. I said home, not that old house."

Maya frowned. Home? House? Past? Present? What did this all mean? Her head ached.

Not releasing her grip, Halmunee bent down to pick up the spoon Maya had dropped earlier and tapped it against Maya until she took it. Before Maya could ask another question, a sharp tug jerked her forward as if she was being dragged behind a race car. Maya screamed, but nothing came out of her mouth. The world blurred around her until, with a jolt, they stopped. A loud clatter rang in her ears. Somewhere, Gizmo barked.

CHAPTER 3

MOTHERS AND DAUGHTERS

"See?" said Halmunee. "Home."

Halmunee then nudged Maya and pointed at the floor. "Yah! What good is bringing back your spoon if you're going to drop it and scratch it up as soon as we get back? Pick it up and bring it to the sink."

Still numb from shock, Maya looked down to where Halmunee pointed. Gizmo was already busy sniffing the spoon and licking up any invisible remnants of patbingsu that lingered behind. Maya lifted her head and looked around, taking in the sight of her familiar old kitchen.

The ice machine hadn't moved from where they had last left it, and the patbingsu in their bowls had shrunk as some of the ice had melted.

Maya tried taking a step forward, but a wave of dizziness and nausea washed over her. A faint aroma of roasted chestnuts hung in the air. She reached out for the countertop to steady herself and slowly lowered herself to the floor. Wrapping her arms around her legs, she rocked back and forth until her breathing steadied.

She lifted her head when Gizmo bumped into her, and after a brief tug-of-war with him she reclaimed the spoon, now slick with dog saliva, and stood up on wobbly legs. Trailing her hand along the countertop, she made her way to the sink and dropped the spoon into it.

Halmunee puttered over and stabbed her finger at a smudge of patbingsu on Maya's shirt.

"How did this happen?"

Shaking her head and making soft clucking sounds, Halmunee licked her thumb and tried to wipe it away.

"Always making a mess when you eat. Come on, give the shirt to me. We need to wash it before the stain sets."

Maya pulled off her shirt. Luckily, the burgundy stain hadn't seeped through to her tank top underneath. Halmunee yanked the shirt from Maya and headed toward the washer and dryer in the garage.

Maya watched as Halmunee opened the door to the garage and leaned forward on her toes, groping for the light switch along the wall. After Halmunee stumbled and almost fell, Maya shook herself out of her stupor.

Everything had changed, but nothing was different. And Mom would kill Maya if anything happened to Halmunee on her watch.

"Wait! I'll do that later!" Maya ran over and grabbed Halmunee's elbow to lead her away from the dark and stuffy garage.

"No," protested Halmunee, struggling against Maya's lead and trying to turn around. "I have to soak it now or else the stain will set. Otherwise what will Appa wear to work tomorrow?"

Maya couldn't tell if by "Appa" Halmunee meant Maya's father, her mom's father, or Halmunee's own father. But it didn't matter. Halmunee was slipping. She'd already forgotten that it was Maya's shirt she was holding in her hands. And the increasing confusion and anger in her voice told Maya that Halmunee needed some rest. She was mixing up the past and the present.

"Don't worry." Maya kept her voice low and soothing as she took her shirt from Halmunee. "As soon as I get you settled in your bed for a nice nap, I promise I'll take care of the shirt right away."

Maya had so many questions about what had just happened, but she knew that she wouldn't get a single answer until Halmunee was assured that the shirt had been treated with stain remover and put in the washer. Priorities.

Maya gently led Halmunee to her room and helped her into bed. It was still hot, but Halmunee pulled the quilt up to her chin and was soon snoring away.

Maya picked up the photo on the dresser and stared at it. She was starting to realize that there was a lot she didn't know about Halmunee.

Like, for example, her ability to travel back in time. That was kind of a big one.

Maya put the photo back in its place and tiptoed out of Halmunee's bedroom and down the stairs to the living room. She collapsed on her bamboo mat with Gizmo and stared up at the faint cracks in the ceiling.

Now what?

She had wanted to be left alone earlier. But now there was nothing she wanted less.

She wanted Halmunee to be awake and lucid. She wanted to know what had just happened. She wanted to know if it had all been real.

She wanted answers.

Running her fingers through Gizmo's soft fur, she debated what to do next.

Should she say anything about this to Mom? She didn't want to frighten or worry Mom unnecessarily. And maybe this was all in her head. Would that be worse, if she were going crazy?

Or maybe Halmunee had an explanation for all of this. Though Maya couldn't think of any explanation that made sense.

Finally, Maya decided to call Mom. She wouldn't tell her everything at first. Maybe just test the waters. A lot would depend on what kind of mood she was in.

Mom picked up on the second ring. She always was quick to answer the phone and start the conversation with an assumption that something was wrong.

"Maya? What is it? Everything okay?"

"Hi, Mom. Yeah, everything's fine."

The reassuring lie slipped out before Maya knew it. She wished she could start the conversation over. This already wasn't going well.

"I'm really swamped right now, so I can't talk too long." Working at a law firm, Mom was busy most days. "Where's Halmunee?"

"She's taking a nap."

"How's she doing?"

"Fine," said Maya. "But she was talking about Appa a few minutes ago. I couldn't tell who she meant—her father or Harabujee. Or maybe Dad? Did she know Dad well?"

Maya tried to keep the eagerness out of her voice. She knew Mom was reluctant to answer questions about Dad. But Maya couldn't help herself. She used any excuse to bring him up with Mom, hoping for any new tidbits of information. He had died when Maya was only three, so she couldn't even remember him. She tried piecing him together from the details she'd slowly dug out of Mom, but he was like a jigsaw puzzle with half the pieces missing. And those pieces were being hoarded and hidden by Mom.

"Don't worry about it. It doesn't matter," Mom said. "Either way, this just means Halmunee's getting more confused."

"But—"

"Look, Maya, I have to finish preparing for a meeting I have in a few minutes. Was there another reason you called?"

"No. Not really." Maya mentally kicked herself. She had gotten sidetracked asking about Dad. She really wanted to say something about what had happened with Halmunee. Otherwise, what was the point of this call?

Trying to sound casual, she said, "Halmunee wanted patbingsu and found an old ice machine in the garage."

"She really needs to stop digging around in the garage so much," said Mom. "One of these days she's going to fall or something's going to fall on her and I'm not going to let that happen. I'll talk to her about it later. Just make sure you clean everything up. Okay? I'll see you soon."

Maya's mouth was so dry, her tongue was like sandpaper against the roof of her mouth. She steeled herself to continue, despite her mom's clear wish she'd hang up. "When we were eating, something kind of weird happened."

"Hmm? Oh yeah?" Mom was already halfway checked out of the conversation. Maya could hear her long nails clacking against the keyboard.

Maya fought back the urge to scream to get Mom's attention and instead cleared her throat and spoke louder. "Something kind of weird happened while we were eating. Halmunee got really nostalgic. It was for a time when you, Halmunee, and Harabujee were all eating patbingsu out in the backyard when you were really little."

"When I ate patbingsu? With Halmunee and Harabujee?" Still typing, Mom was repeating after Maya to buy some time to catch up to the conversation.

"Yeah. I thought it might ring a bell with you."

"I don't know. That doesn't sound familiar."

Mom had been really young, maybe two or three, in that moment in time, but Maya kept prodding. "It was like I was there with you all. You had pigtails and a white dress with balloons on it. You and Harabujee fought Halmunee over the patbingsu with your spoons."

The clicking of the keyboard stopped and Mom let out a long sigh that whistled through the phone.

"Oh, I'd almost forgotten. He loved patbingsu so much. Whenever it got so hot that not even lying on the big bamboo mat helped cool us down, he'd announce that it was perfect weather for patbingsu. And just like that, it was like it was ten degrees cooler." After a small cough, Mom's wistful remembrance ended and she was back to her usual no-nonsense tone. "But no point in obsessing about the past. Nothing good comes from that. Anyways, it sounds like you had a good time with Halmunee?"

"Yeah," said Maya slowly. "I just thought you might have had moments like that with Halmunee."

Mom snorted. "No. You know I love Halmunee, but we don't really talk that much about stuff like that. Our relationship is . . . complicated. We're not a typical mother-and-daughter pair. But I'm glad you're close. It's nice of you to listen to her stories and keep her company."

Mom did take very good care of Halmunee, but even Maya had noticed a certain distance between them. Maya wasn't sure if it was the clash of their strong personalities—so different, yet similarly stubborn—or the strain of taking care of Halmunee that was to blame. Maybe Mom and Halmunee just had one of those mother-daughter relationships that was destined to be tense.

Things usually weren't smooth between them. Even that first day Halmunee had arrived had been filled with stress and awkwardness instead of joy and excitement. Maya had come back from her best friend Jada's house to find Mom shaking with frustration at Halmunee's vague answers as to how she had arrived and why she was there. Halmunee just kept saying that it was time for her visit. Maya had retreated to her room to avoid any misdirected anger. It wasn't until the next day that Maya was able to fully enjoy the excitement of having a bigger family than just her and Mom.

"Oh, hold on a second." Maya couldn't tell if Mom was talking to her or to someone in the office, but then Mom said, "Maya, I have to go. They're calling me for the meeting. I'll be home in a couple hours."

Maya forced a cheerful and breezy response. "Sounds great! See you soon!"

"Bye, Maya. Love you."

"Bye. Love you too."

Nudging Gizmo off her lap, Maya ended the call and stood up.

This process of unraveling information from others was as strange and uncomfortable as putting on a pair of shoes that weren't your own.

It looked like she would just have to wait until Halmunee woke up to get some facts straight.

CHAPTER 4

SERIOUS FRIEND COUNSELING

But Maya didn't get her answers that day.

Halmunee woke up cranky and disoriented—and as soon as Mom came home, Halmunee got even more confused. With a yelp, she shut her bedroom door and refused to come out. This wasn't that uncommon. Lately Halmunee often got confused around dinnertime and thought she was in the wrong house with the wrong family. And by the time they managed to convince her to come downstairs to eat, Mom was hungry, tired, and just as irritable as Halmunee.

Tonight, after everyone was finally seated at the table, Halmunee picked at the pizza slice on her plate and muttered, "So unhealthy and greasy. This isn't proper food. Maya needs something better."

Mom stiffened. Maya knew this would set Mom off. When it was just Mom and Maya, dinner was a time for catching up on each other's days or for comfortable silence. But now, Halmunee frequently challenged Mom's decisions. Some of it was due to Halmunee's increasing forgetfulness and confusion, but most of it seemed to be done purposefully, with tension sparking in the air between them.

"I'm sorry I didn't have time to make a home-cooked meal," Mom said icily. "I was busy working at a full-time, demanding job to make enough money to support this family and pay all of the bills. I don't even have time or energy for any kind of social life. You remember what that's like."

"Family and health should come first," said Halmunee. "It's just like I told your father yesterday."

Maya looked up to correct her grandmother, but Mom shook her head. Sometimes they tried explaining things to Halmunee when she got mixed up, and some of those times she'd understand. But that was getting rarer, and Mom was trying less. Often it was just easier to ignore the odd comments and continue on.

Maya finished her dinner as silently and quickly as possible, and then jumped up to clear the table. She washed their plates by hand, since neither Mom nor Halmunee trusted the dishwasher to do a thorough-enough job.

Needing to get out of the house, she texted her best friend to see if she could hang out. Jada was back from her trip to visit family in Jamaica, but she was stuck at home babysitting her younger brothers. She told Maya to come over. They were both in need of an escape from their families.

Maya waited until Halmunee was quiet in her room and Mom was relaxing on the sofa with a glass of wine in her hand, her feet on the coffee table, and Gizmo snoring on her lap.

"I'm going to Jada's," said Maya.

Mom didn't even look away from the television as she browsed through her saved shows. "One hour. I want you back before it gets dark."

Maya picked up her keys. Gizmo sat up at the sound and watched her with his head tilted to the side and sad eyes begging her to stay. But she needed to get out of the house and away from her family. She wanted something that felt real and normal at that moment.

Racing against the setting sun, Maya ran straight to her friend's house, her long black hair streaming behind her. After the uncomfortable pizza dinner, it felt good to shake everything loose and leave it all behind. Maya swerved off the sidewalk, avoiding the sprinklers going off as neighbors fought to maintain lush, green lawns in the desert climate of southern California.

Jada lived only a block away. Maya texted her as she walked up to the front door, and the door opened silently. Jada grinned and beckoned her inside. She looked a little taller, and her already deep complexion had darkened several shades after her summer in Jamaica. She was in her pajamas with her hair wrapped up.

"Are they asleep?" Maya whispered.

Jada shrugged. "Maybe. Maybe not. But they won't bother us." She tilted her head toward the stairs behind her and raised her voice. "Because they know not to get out of bed or they'll get in big trouble!"

Upstairs, loud footsteps raced to the other side of the house. A door slammed shut and soft giggles faded away.

Maya slipped off her shoes. She knew she didn't have to take off her shoes like at her own house, but it felt too weird keeping them on inside. Since everyone was apparently still awake, Maya followed

Jada's cue and raised her voice to a normal level as they walked over to the living room.

"You don't know how good it feels to be somewhere with air conditioning. Can I just move in with you and live here for the rest of the summer?"

"Sure, My. If you can handle living with my brothers."

Maya felt the tension in her body melt away. It was almost like she was an entirely different Maya when she was around Jada and their other friends. Family Maya was a good and respectful daughter who never made any trouble or loud noise. But Friend Maya talked freely and laughed loudly. She was never afraid to ask questions and sought answers to the most mundane and the most fantastic of topics. She even sat differently, one leg tucked under her as she slumped comfortably against the pillows in a low, curved pose that would make Mom and Halmunee cringe.

Jada plopped onto the sofa and held out a plate of cookies. Maya couldn't resist Jada's famous salty double chocolate chip cookies, or SDC cookies as they liked to call them, and took two of them. It was a recipe that Jada had learned from her dad. Maya envied that Jada had that kind of tradition with her father and felt a slight pang of jealousy every time she ate a delicious SDC cookie. They had just the right amount of sea salt on top that contrasted perfectly with the generous serving of bittersweet chocolate chips. Jada liked to say that they were salty and sweet, just like her.

"Are you going to sleep soon too?" asked Maya. "It's early, but you could have just told me and I wouldn't have come over."

"Nah," said Jada, turning on the television. "I just got into my pajamas to encourage the little brats to get ready for bed. Besides, I'm comfy and it's not like I can go anywhere tonight while I'm watching them. What's up? You sounded stressed before."

With her mouth half full, Maya mumbled, "How can I sound stressed over text?"

Jada looked at Maya and arched a single eyebrow. "Please. I've known you forever. I can tell." Jada wiped the cookie crumbs off her hands, took a bottle of turquoise nail polish from a bin on the coffee table, and started painting her toenails.

"Is it about David?" Jada poked Maya with an elbow and made a funny face.

Maya poked her back. "No, it's not about David." Her cheeks flushed as she said his name. "Cute color," she added as she tried to change the subject.

"Thanks," said Jada. "Are you *sure* it's not about David?"

Maya never should have told Jada about her crush. It wasn't a big deal. Almost every girl in their class had had a crush on him. Well, not Jada.

"No," said Maya. "It really isn't!"

"So, what's going on then? Is it your mom again? Or your grandmother?"

Maya loved how well Jada knew her—both Family Maya and Friend Maya. Of course, Jada couldn't resist teasing and making jokes, but she always knew when Maya needed some serious friend counseling.

Maya stared at her best friend and debated how much to tell her. She had never kept secrets from her before, but nothing really compared to "I either time-traveled to the past with my grandmother or I'm having some serious hallucinations."

Maya opened her mouth to answer Jada's question, then abruptly shut it. Something had shifted. Even though she thought she had left Family Maya at home, she hadn't. Family Maya and Friend Maya fought over their respective territories until Maya decided on a middle ground.

"I, uh, I think my grandmother shared something with me that she hasn't shared with anyone else. Not even my mom. But I don't know if it's real or not. I mean, what she shared with me. And I don't want to say something and worry my mom about it if it's not real. I'm sorry, does any of that make any sense?"

"Family stuff." Jada nodded. "It's always the worst." She leaned in closer. "So, what was it? Some juicy big secret? You're actually descendants of Korean royalty? You have a long-lost sister?"

"What? No. Nothing like that."

"Well, what is it then?"

"I can't really say. I mean, I don't want to say anything about it because it could be nothing, and I don't want to make a big deal out of it and everything."

"Come on," said Jada. "Now tell me for real."

"I . . . I can't tell you."

"Seriously?"

Feeling guilty for keeping a secret from her best friend, Maya nodded.

"Oh." Jada looked at her with a strange expression on her face before turning back to the television. "Okay. I get it."

They sat in silence. Family Maya smugly settled over Maya like an old sweater that was both comforting and itchy.

Maya wanted to tell Jada everything, but she didn't know if it was the right thing to do at this point. And she had no clue how she would even begin telling the truth about what had happened that day. She couldn't even bring herself to tell Mom.

Maya jumped up and nervously ran her fingers through her hair. She just wanted this day to end. It had been one tense moment followed by another.

"Thanks for the cookies. I should head back. My mom said to be home before it gets dark."

"Okay." Jada shrugged, then got up and walked Maya to the door.

The streetlights were beginning to flicker on, though they were barely noticeable in the orange haze of the early evening light. The air was still heavy and warm, but it felt nice after being inside Jada's cold house.

As Maya walked down the front steps, Jada called out to her.

"My, don't worry so much. Just talk to your grandmother some more and see if you can confirm it yourself. And if you ever need help, I'm always here."

Maya knew that Jada meant that both symbolically and literally. Jada would listen to anything Maya had to say and sympathize with her, but she also was an amazing researcher and could find out anything, given enough time on her computer. Well, almost anything. Jada hadn't been able to find anything about Maya's father when Maya had asked her to look years ago.

The terrible awkward feeling between the two best friends disappeared, and Maya smiled at Jada. "Thanks, Jay." She waved goodbye and then ran down the street.

Yes. That's what she'd do. She wouldn't say anything to Mom just now. That would only stress Mom out further or give her a reason to get angry at Halmunee again. Instead, Maya would wait to talk to Halmunee first and hopefully get some sort of solid evidence one way or another.

Maya felt much better now that she had a plan. With a light bounce in her step, she slipped back into her house just a minute before Mom's one-hour deadline.

CHAPTER 5

DOENJANG JJIGAE

"Maya!"

The next morning a voice pierced through Maya's deep, dreamless sleep. With a long yawn, she rolled over to squint at the clock on her nightstand.

It was still early. Early for Maya, at least.

She wasn't a morning person, and she'd been enjoying being able to sleep in without school or her summer program to worry about. She didn't have much more time with this bliss since school would start soon, but Halmunee either didn't know or didn't care. Or both.

"Maya!" she called out again. "Come down and eat."

Maya sat on the edge of her bed until she felt like she had enough energy to get up. As she pulled open her door, she smelled something seeping through the house—strangely pungent, yet intriguing. Maya stumbled down the stairs and let her nose lead her to the kitchen.

Halmunee stood bathed in steam that was curling up from an

earthenware pot on the stovetop. She had somehow managed to find the only apron in the house and had tied it tight around her frail form.

Gizmo sat on the kitchen floor just behind her, panting. His head was tilted back and he was begging for a taste of whatever was filling the kitchen with that intense smell. He barely looked Maya's way before returning to his vigil.

Halmunee turned to yell over her shoulder again, then stopped and smiled when she saw Maya.

"Finally. You're awake. Come in and sit."

Still groggy, Maya slumped onto a stool at the counter. The heat of the stove made her pull back a little. How did Halmunee stand it?

Something about this scenario made her a little nervous, like an itch on her back that she couldn't quite reach. It took her sleepy mind longer than usual to figure it out, and it was only as she eyed the flickering flame under the pot that she realized what it was.

Halmunee was cooking on the gas range by herself.

For a few seconds, Maya debated whether she should say something to Mom about this when she got home. Mom had never explicitly forbidden Halmunee from cooking by herself, but she often shooed her away from the stove when it was lit. Even though Halmunee seemed fine right now, Maya didn't know when a good moment might turn into a bad moment. And the bad moments would surely increase; she'd only become more unpredictable and unreliable over time.

Maybe Maya would bring it up with Mom later, after work. And maybe, by then, she'd have more information about what had happened the previous day. She could use the rest of the day to talk to

Halmunee and patiently draw out the truth from her.

With her mind made up, she turned her attention back to the bubbling stew in the pot and pointed at it.

"That smells good. What is it?"

"It's doenjang jjigae." Halmunee took a sip of the stew and smacked her lips together a few times before reaching for more salt. "It's filled with things that are good for you. Squash. Radish. Tofu. Fermented soybean."

Maya wrinkled her nose. "For breakfast? That seems wrong." But her stomach betrayed her brain and grumbled with hunger.

"Of course," said Halmunee. "What else would you eat for breakfast?"

Maya shrugged. "Nothing usually. I'm either waking up late or running late for some other reason. Maybe a bagel or a donut."

Halmunee shook her head in disapproval. "How can you start your day right and do well in school if you don't have proper nutrition in your stomach? In Korea, there's no difference between breakfast and any other meal in the type of food you eat. We eat soup and rice and even fish. What matters most is that you eat something good and filling to start your day."

Not wanting to get bogged down in an argument about eating better and definitely not wanting to eat fish for breakfast, Maya said, "I didn't realize we had all the ingredients for this."

Halmunee shrugged. "Some of this you already had. Other things I got from the market."

Maya frowned as she pieced together what Halmunee was saying.

"The market? When did you go? By yourself?"

Halmunee ignored Maya's questions and pulled on a pair of oven mitts before moving the pot to the trivet on the counter. "Don't touch. It's hot. Go and get the kimchi out of the fridge."

Kimchi in the morning? Maya shuddered at the thought.

The rice cooker chirped. Halmunee rushed over to it, calling over her shoulder, "Kimchi! Spoons! Chopsticks!"

Deciding to be a good granddaughter and respectful to her elder, Family Maya went to the refrigerator and pulled out the large container of kimchi that Halmunee had made a couple weeks back. She was still skeptical that she'd have any appetite for kimchi this early in the day. But again, her stomach voiced its excitement as soon as she opened the top and the familiar strong aroma hit her nose. Even though Mom's Korean cooking was limited and they went out to eat in Koreatown only a few times a year, there was something about kimchi that just felt like home to Maya.

Halmunee ladled the jjigae into two bowls and placed one in front of Maya. The kimchi and a large bowl of rice sat on the counter between them. Halmunee waved her spoon in the air. "Eat, eat."

As if she didn't trust that Maya would start eating, Halmunee picked up the rice and dumped large spoonfuls into Maya's bowl of jjigae.

"Okay, okay!" Maya took her bowl back from Halmunee and began to eat.

And then there were no more words exchanged between them, because Maya was lost in the spicy, tangy flavors of the jjigae. Blowing hot air between her teeth, she chomped on the softened pieces of zucchini and radish. Her tongue seemed to remember the flavors from the few Korean meals of her past, and something deep within her was sated as she slurped up the comforting stew.

Her eyes darted to the kimchi in front of her and she eagerly picked up a few thick squares of the fermented, spicy cabbage. The kimchi was so fresh and light, the juices it was soaking in could be spooned up for a refreshing cold soup—which was exactly what Maya did.

Maya was so distracted by the food, she forgot about everything else. Halmunee's cool hand on her wrist startled her. With a slight tremor in her other hand, Halmunee lifted a spoonful of the jjigae to her mouth, the steam fogging up her thin-rimmed glasses. As she took her first taste, she smiled at Maya.

Before Maya could say anything, her stomach lurched and she was pulled back in time once again. She tried to keep calm and focus on Halmunee's grip on her wrist as she was bombarded with different smells and images like before. She took a deep breath, and suddenly her feet landed on solid ground and the world stopped spinning.

A slurping sound next to Maya drew her attention. Halmunee was happily eating the last bits of jjigae from her spoon.

How did she manage to make the trip without spilling anything?

Luckily, Maya had dropped her own spoon into her bowl when she realized what was happening, managing to avoid another stained shirt.

Turning away from Halmunee, Maya slowly took in her new surroundings. The room they stood in was small and old-fashioned. It was sparsely furnished compared to her home, but the pieces of furniture were of good quality and everything was impeccably clean. A few Korean paintings and scrolls decorated the otherwise plain walls, and porcelain vases and bowls rested atop large bureaus covered with ornate metalware and carvings. In the center of the room, there was a low wooden table with steaming bowls of doenjang jjigae. Almost every other inch of the table was covered in smaller bowls of rice and the tasty side dishes that Maya recognized as banchan.

Seated on the floor around the table were a gangly girl with bobbed hair and a stern older woman in a hanbok, her hair pulled back into a low bun.

"Again?" Maya stared at Halmunee until she met her gaze. "Are you going to tell me what's going on this time?"

Halmunee's eyes widened innocently. For a second, Maya wondered if her grandmother had forgotten who she was and where they were—until Halmunee shushed her. "Quiet. I can't hear."

It felt like they were watching a movie and Halmunee was telling her to be quiet so she could focus on the actors on the big screen. Maya opened her mouth to ask another question, but the older woman slammed her hand on the table, making Maya jump and the silverware and bowls clatter.

"Hyun Suk, why did you do this, huh?" The woman's voice was edged with steel, and Maya couldn't help but stand taller. It often took a little time for her to switch to Family Maya with her Korean brain, but, even if she hadn't been able to understand the words themselves, Maya recognized the tone. She felt like she was the one being reprimanded. It didn't help that her nerves were already frayed from the trip.

Maya turned her attention to the teenage girl. Hyun Suk? But that was Halmunee's name. Maya stared at the girl and began to see the features of her grandmother in her face. She couldn't believe that

Halmunee had ever been so young, probably the same age as Maya was at that moment. Next, she turned to the older woman.

So, this is my great-grandmother, thought Maya.

Apparently, very intimidating mothers ran in her family. She saw the resemblance to Halmunee in her great-grandmother, with the same eyes and mouth, but there was also a deep crease between her eyebrows and more lines etched across her great-grandmother's face. Maya did some quick math to figure out they were probably in the 1960s, not that long after the Korean War. This was a woman who had lived a harder life than Maya could ever know, one who had been tasked with keeping her family alive during a war that tore her country in half. Maya couldn't help but admire this woman even if she was frightened by her at the same time.

Hyun Suk squirmed in her seat but didn't answer. She kept her head bowed low and avoided making eye contact with her mother. Her posture shouted meekness and obedience, but her hands were balled up tight into fists under the table.

"How could you do this?"

Hyun Suk remained silent as her mother raged on.

"You're too old for this. You're almost a woman. Do you know how shameful your behavior was? How bad it makes you look? How bad it makes your family look?"

Family Maya knew these weren't questions that Hyun Suk was expected to answer. That would be a rookie mistake. These were the type of rhetorical questions that were just meant to further shame and punish, pointing out great disappointments and failures. A surefire way to make the situation worse was to try to provide answers and then be accused of talking back.

Maya looked closer at Hyun Suk. A dark blue crescent moon cradled her left eye, and deep red scratches ran across her cheeks and arms. Maya's eyes grew big and her mouth dropped open in shock.

Hyun Suk had been in a fight!

Maya couldn't believe it. While she wouldn't have been surprised to hear that Mom had gotten in a fight or two at school when she was young, she never would have thought that of Halmunee. It was still hard to imagine Halmunee had ever been such a young and fierce girl.

Hyun Suk's mother continued, "A school is a place for learning, not playing around and fighting. And your cousin is older than you by five months. She is your elder and you should treat her with the proper respect."

Hyun Suk finally couldn't sit still; she burst out, "Soon Mi eonni doesn't deserve my respect!" Hyun Suk's face was red with anger and her fists slammed against her crossed legs. She may have used the respectful term *eonni*, older sister, after Soon Mi's name, but she spit it out as if it was dirt on her tongue. "She called me a freak! She called you a freak! She said that you killed one of your cousins! She said our entire family was crazy and we all deserved to be locked up in an asylum. She deserved worse than what I gave her."

Hyun Suk clamped her mouth shut with her hands.

Hyun Suk's mother leaned back and blinked in surprise. "What do you mean? What happened? Tell me the truth."

Hyun Suk lowered her hands from her face. Her cheeks were still flushed with anger.

"She said that we're all lying about our abilities. That we're either big liars or crazy freaks. She didn't believe me. So I said that she was just being jealous because my family is strong while hers is weak. And then she pushed me. She hit me first!"

A strained silence passed, interrupted by Hyun Suk's frequent sniffs as she wiped away the tears spilling down her cheeks.

When Hyun Suk's mother spoke, it was with a softer and sadder tone than before.

"Soon Mi is just like her omma, your imo. Bad temper and too stubborn. Your imo has always been upset that our omma's power passed on to me and my children, and not her. And so now she's telling her children that it's all a lie. That it doesn't exist. She's turned her back on our family. But that still doesn't give you an excuse to fight with Soon Mi. Or with anyone else, for that matter."

Hyun Suk stared at her mother. All anger had vanished from her face and she sat quietly, as though she didn't want to disturb her mother's train of thought.

"From this point on, you don't talk with anyone about what we can do," her mother said. "Not even your friends or cousins. Not everyone will understand or want to understand. And what we do can be very dangerous."

Hyun Suk looked up at her mother, a question in her eyes that she refused to voice. But Hyun Suk didn't need to say it. Her mother knew.

"I didn't kill my cousin," said Hyun Suk's mother. "I hope you know better than to believe that lie."

"Yes." Hyun Suk bowed her head respectfully to her mother.

"But I am responsible for her disappearance."

Hyun Suk gasped and her eyes grew large.

Her mother reached out to hold her hand and continued in a soft but stern voice. "I want you to listen carefully to me," she said. "This is a very important lesson, and I never want you to make the same mistake that I did—the same mistake that many of our ancestors have made, I later learned. Even with the lessons of our past, pride can still tempt us to do what we know is wrong. Remember when I first taught you how to travel back, I said to never ever try to travel to the future?"

"Yes," said Hyun Suk. "You said that there is only one past, but there is never just one future."

"That's right. A decision made in the present can result in a completely different future, and there is an infinite number of possible futures."

"But what about inyeon?" asked Hyun Suk.

Inyeon.

There was that word again. Maya made a mental note to add this word to her journal.

"Yes," said Hyun Suk's mother. "All relationships, even fleeting moments, are tied together as part of our destiny. But that doesn't mean the same thing across all our futures. It's very rare for some things to be destined like that. Just think, when you go backward in time, you go as a visitor. You can't change what has already happened. But when you travel to the future, you're changing everything. You're picking a set path that you're now tied to. You can't go back anymore because that future is now your present. Understand?"

Hyun Suk solemnly nodded.

"Well, that is what caused my cousin's disappearance. We were young and reckless and constantly testing our abilities," continued

Hyun Suk's mother. "Our families told us that we were the strongest travelers known in recent generations, and we got overconfident. And one day I dared my cousin to travel to the future."

Hyun Suk gasped. "What happened?"

"She never came back. She was lost in time. We don't know where or when she traveled to." The crease between her eyebrows deepened. "We were too proud. We were arrogant! I tried going back to see if I could change things. If I could stop myself from making that stupid dare. But I couldn't. I found out later that several members of our family in past generations have been lost in time and were never heard from again. So next time Soon Mi says anything bad about you or our family, ignore her. Don't let yourself get angry or overly confident. Now finish your breakfast."

Hyun Suk picked up her spoon and dug into the jjigae before her. Her face was still red and her eyes were still puffy, but she ate with a renewed energy while peeking at her mother, as if viewing her in a new light.

Hyun Suk's mother watched her daughter with a strange expression on her face—the same sad and melancholy expression that Halmunee now had as she watched the scene unfold from her past.

Maya wondered how many times Halmunee had visited this fight and how long it had been since she'd last talked with her mother. Did watching these moments with long-dead loved ones help ease the pain of loss or worsen it? After all, it appeared that Halmunee could only relive old memories. She couldn't create new ones with her own mother or Harabujee. And Maya worried that one day Halmunee would become too sick to make any new memories at all.

As Hyun Suk finished the last of her jjigae, Halmunee cleared her throat and reached for Maya's hand.

"It's time."

Maya was better prepared for the pull back to the present this time. She tried to breathe evenly as the world blurred around her and the familiar scent of roasting chestnuts filled the air.

CHAPTER 6

THE THEATER

"Give me your bowl and I'll warm it up for you," said Halmunee, rising from her stool.

Maya reached out to stop Halmunee and pull her back to her seat. She took Halmunee's thin, wrinkled hand in her own and gave it a gentle squeeze.

"Halmunee, what is this?" she asked softly. "I don't need any more food. I need some answers. Please. What's going on?"

Halmunee looked up at Maya. She stared for so long that Maya worried that she was slipping away again, already forgetting where they had been and what they had been doing. But just as Maya was about to give up hope and start clearing the dishes, Halmunee spoke, her voice clear and steady.

"Ever since I was little girl, I've had two special gifts passed down to me from my mother. Not everyone in our family is blessed with these gifts, and it's unpredictable who will have them. But having them isn't enough. You need to be taught how to use them. The first gift is that I am an excellent cook. Nobody's dishes can beat mine. Once you taste my food, no other version will ever satisfy you again. Any Korean food, I can make. No dish is too complicated for me. And I always know how to find the best ingredients."

Modesty was not one of Halmunee's strengths.

"And the second gift?" asked Maya.

"The second gift is that I can use my strength in the kitchen to bring back memories." Halmunee paused and shook her head. "No, that's not quite the right way to describe it. I mean that I can return to moments in the past. The smells and tastes of the food I make can awaken the old memories buried deep in here and here." She tapped her head and then placed her hand over her heart. "And then I can retrace my footsteps back to an exact day and hour."

"So . . . you can time-travel?" asked Maya.

"It's like time travel, but not like it. When I go back to those moments, I'm watching the actual people and actual events that once happened. But I'm not an actual part of that moment. I can only watch. It's like I'm in the audience of a . . ." Halmunee paused as she tried to find the word that evaded her.

"A movie theater," suggested Maya. She thought back to that moment at the beginning of their last trip, when Halmunee had shushed her and it had felt like they were watching a movie.

Halmunee nodded. "Yes. Exactly. So, you see, you can't talk with anyone and you can't change anything that already happened in the past."

Maya scrunched up her face like she was trying to do long division in her head, keeping track of all the things she'd seen and all the things Halmunee had just said.

"Okay. But there's one thing I still don't get. If we're not technically in the past, then where are we? What does it look like when we leave?"

Halmunee sighed. "I'm not explaining it well. My omma did a much better job when she first showed me. Let me try again."

Even with Halmunee's confused and distorted way of thinking at times, Maya was usually able to pick up on her train of thought pretty quickly and was able to meet her in the middle. It was a level of connection that Maya used to have with her mom. Now, Maya was having a hard time following Halmunee's explanation.

Halmunee looked around and pointed at Maya's journal. "Give me your notebook and get me a pen. I'll show it to you."

Maya hesitated. She never let anyone else write in her journal. But she didn't want to miss an opportunity to learn the truth, so she retrieved her journal and opened it to a blank page before sliding it across to Halmunee.

Halmunee took Maya's journal and began drawing the interior layout of a building from above, with multiple long hallways extending out like the legs of a spider. Every inch or so down the hallway, Halmunee drew an entrance that led to a large room.

"Think of our trips back as going to a movie theater," said Halmunee.

Maya nodded. This analogy made a lot of sense to her already.

"Each moment in the past is its own movie," said Halmunee. "And each time we go back, we choose to go inside a different room to watch a showing of a different movie."

Halmunee drew a small patbingsu in one of the rooms extending out from a hallway and a bowl of jjigae in another. "So, each time I cook, smell, or taste something tied to a food from a specific

memory, I can make that connection. I can find that movie. Behind this door is the patbingsu 'movie,' and behind this other door is the jjigae 'movie.' And with each trip, we can only watch. We can't change the movie. It's already been filmed. Get it?"

Maya nodded slowly. "I think I get it." She still needed more time to think about everything and let it sink in. It was a lot of information being thrown at her and she couldn't remember if Halmunee had answered all of her questions. At least the comparison to a movie theater had made some kind of sense to her. "Who else can do this? Can Mom?"

"Well, you know how talents are," said Halmunee. "Sometimes things skip around in families. There's no guarantee who will get it."

"What about Harabujee? Did he know?"

"This is not something to go around telling other people. You saw what happened to me before with Soon Mi. We used to be very close friends when we were little, but we barely spoke to each other after that incident. Who would believe this?"

Halmunee shut the journal and rose unsteadily to her feet.

"No. Some things are not meant to be and are better left unknown. It's easier that way."

Maya persisted. "But you didn't tell anyone after that? Not even Harabujee? Mom? No one? Didn't you want to tell someone?"

No wonder Mom and Halmunee didn't get along. There was a huge canyon of secrets separating them.

Maya couldn't imagine holding onto such a great secret for so long. An entire lifetime.

Halmunee smiled and patted Maya's cheek. "I tell you now." She turned and headed to the refrigerator. "Now go and set the table and I'll make you a big meal. It's not often you and your family get to visit us for lunch nowadays."

Frowning, Maya followed Halmunee and stopped her. "Who are you talking about? And it's only nine o'clock. We were just having breakfast. Don't you remember? The doenjang jjigae?" She gestured to the now-cold bowls on the table.

Halmunee stared blankly at Maya and then at the sink. A crease deepened between her brows as the corners of her mouth pulled down. At that moment, Halmunee looked just like Hyun Suk's mother from that moment they'd visited.

A small part of Maya was secretly thrilled that she noticed this; that she now knew what her great-grandmother looked like and could make these kinds of mundane observations. Family Maya fed greedily on this new information and almost squeaked in excitement before remembering herself.

"I know that," said Halmunee, cutting into Maya's thoughts. "Of course I remember. I'm just tired. I need some rest. You can take care of the dishes, right?"

Maya nodded, but Halmunee had already turned away. By the time a quiet "yes" had slipped out of her mouth, Halmunee was out of earshot, slowly climbing the stairs one at a time.

Maya didn't want to overly tax Halmunee, but she so desperately wanted to know more about her family in Korea. She could try asking Mom, but she never got much out of her. She wondered if Mom had been close with her own grandmother. They both seemed like very strong and determined women.

Maya smiled to herself. Another familial connection she had made.

CHAPTER 7

BIRTHDAY MIYEOK-GUK

Not long after their doenjang jjigae trip, just after Labor Day, Maya started seventh grade. It was already much harder than sixth. Maya was overwhelmed with tons of homework from the very first day, and she hadn't had a chance to go on any more trips with Halmunee. By the time she got home from school Halmunee was often taking her afternoon nap. By the time she woke up, Maya was either knee-deep in her homework or Mom was home from work.

As if Maya wasn't busy enough, her history teacher, Ms. Fairley, announced that 50 percent of their final grade would depend on a big project that would take up almost the entire semester.

Ms. Fairley had to raise her voice to be heard over the students' complaints. "You will be working in groups of four, and your group must pick a year from the twentieth century and prepare a magazine covering the main events from that year. The magazine must be at least thirty pages. You will also have to do a fifteen-minute presentation of your magazine at the end of the school year. If you can't find a group to join, I will assign you to one."

Maya immediately turned around in her seat to face Jada, and Jada nodded back at her.

Everyone else was settling into their groups. Maya noticed that her crush, David, had a flock of girls trying to join his team. She turned her attention back to Jada, who was grinning at her.

"We still need a third person," said Maya, hoping to distract Jada from teasing her about David again.

Maya looked around the classroom and made eye contact with Izzy, who sat a couple rows away from them. Izzy and her best friend, Emma, were already seated together. Izzy and Jada had been going to the same dance class for the past two years, and Maya knew that Jada liked Emma. This would be the perfect excuse to get them to spend more time together. Izzy nodded and motioned for Maya and Jada to join them.

The students grouped together for the rest of the period to start planning their magazine. Izzy immediately assumed the role of leader for their group. She opened her notebook and started writing notes.

"So I'll do the editing and formatting," said Izzy. "And Jada and Emma, you guys want to be in charge of research and writing?"

Maya grinned at Jada. "That's a great idea."

"Okay," said Emma.

Jada shrugged. "Sure." But Maya could tell Jada was just trying to play it cool, because a slight flush was spreading across her cheeks.

"And Maya, you should obviously do the illustrations and graphics, since you're the only one of us who can draw anything more than a stick figure."

"Okay." Maya was happy having a task best suited for her. She could spend hours drawing and designing stuff.

When Maya came home from school a few hours later, she was surprised to see Halmunee awake and in the kitchen. Halmunee greeted her with a steaming bowl of soup.

"Sit and eat." Halmunee nudged the bowl closer to Maya and handed her a spoon.

"Now? What's this?"

Halmunee poured another bowl of soup for herself and scooped up two steaming spoonfuls of freshly cooked rice that she added to both their bowls.

"This is a very special soup," said Halmunee. "This is miyeok-guk. Birthday soup. Every birthday we eat miyeok-guk. And sometimes on other holidays too."

Maya frowned. She'd never eaten this soup for any of her birthdays, and she couldn't remember seeing this on the menus of the Korean restaurants she'd eaten at. She wondered what other special Korean traditions she had been missing out on.

"Why is it eaten on birthdays?" asked Maya.

"Because it's eaten by mothers after they've given birth," said Halmunee.

This didn't make any sense to Maya.

"What?"

Halmunee sighed. "I forget how little you remembered. Miyeok-guk is a seaweed soup. It's very good for your health, and so mothers often eat it after giving birth. Because of that, it's a birthday soup. You eat it on your birthday and think of your mother and thank her for bringing you into this world."

Maya turned her attention to the soup and inhaled the savory scents of the broth. The soup was filled with slippery masses of something dark green.

"Quickly," said Halmunee. "Eat it while it's hot."

Maya had eaten seaweed with California rolls and cucumber rolls at sushi restaurants, but it was crisp and didn't have much flavor of its own. This seaweed was different. It was so soft, it almost melted in her mouth with the hot, salty broth and rice. An ocean of flavors danced across her tongue, and then the soup settled into a comforting warmth that spread throughout her body.

Maya quickly finished her bowl and asked for seconds. She thought about her mother as she waited. There were so many traditions she had missed out on because Mom simply refused to continue them. But then Maya's frustration vanished as she thought about how hard Mom worked to make sure Maya had everything she wanted and needed. Even things she didn't know she wanted or needed. Like that time a few years ago when Maya was in her peak horse obsession, but when the time came to ride one with a friend she was too scared to get on what felt like a giant beast. A week later, Mom had signed Maya up for riding lessons and told her that she should never let her fears overpower her. That if she really wanted something, she had to fight to overcome any fears and doubts. It took only a few lessons for Maya to be comfortable trotting on a horse. Maya later found out that those evenings she thought Mom was hanging out with new friends, she was really working overtime to pay for those riding lessons.

Just as Maya was about to finish her second bowl, Halmunee reached out to hold her hand. Knowing what was about to happen, Maya quickly grabbed her new sketchbook out of her backpack before they were swept back into the past once again.

Now that this was her third time on the time-traveling roller-coaster, what once was terrifying was now exciting. Maya felt like a pro. She had been barely startled when Halmunee grasped her hand and pulled her into the past or when they landed in a large banquet hall.

Maya wasn't even surprised to see younger versions of her grand-parents again, or the new but vaguely familiar-looking relatives she'd never met before. It helped now to think of it as if she was watching a strange movie, albeit one that was super personal and with no real plot.

Before Maya could ask where and when they were, Halmunee spoke.

"This is my father's birthday party. His sixtieth. A very important birthday, so we had a big party with all of our family and friends. We served all kinds of food that symbolize long life or bring good health. And a Korean birthday of course just isn't complete without miyeok-guk!"

Maya normally hated big events, but this was different. This was her family, a part of her history she had never known. So different from the usual quiet birthday celebrations with just Mom. The festive atmosphere in the room was intoxicating. Maya also loved that she could see everything without having to interact with anyone. She didn't have to worry about making polite conversation over the roar of the crowd and music, or having anyone comment on her outfit, her posture, or how much food she was eating.

Maya couldn't take her eyes off the younger versions of her grandparents—and they couldn't take their eyes off each other. They were so young, probably in their late twenties, and happy.

Everyone was happy. All of Maya's relatives were smiling and laughing at new stories and old jokes.

Maya wished this moment could last forever—and then laughed to herself when she realized that it could. All she needed was Halmunee and some miyeok-guk to take her back anytime she desired.

Halmunee sidled up to Maya and poked her in the side. "We look good, don't we?" Her eyes twinkled. "You forget that we were young once too. Sometimes it's hard for you to remember when you see my wrinkled skin and white hair." She turned back to the younger versions of herself and Harabujee and sighed. "Sometimes it's hard for me to remember too."

Maya searched for another topic to distract Halmunee from getting too depressed and blurted out the first question that popped into her mind. "Why are you wearing a hanbok?"

Halmunee looked down and back over at Maya with a confused look on her face. "I'm not wearing a hanbok. Oh, you mean *that* me!" Her expression cleared, and she laughed as she pointed at the younger version of herself.

From the neck down, Hyun Suk was in traditional Korean wear: a simple but well-cut light blue hanbok with a short, long-sleeved tied top and a long, wide skirt. From the neck up, Hyun Suk was a modern woman for the 1970s. Her hair was teased into a tall updo, her lips were painted a light pink, and her eyeliner had a slight winged edge.

"Yeah," said Maya. "You look amazing, but most of the people here are in modern clothes. I mean, modern at the time." Even Young Soo, sitting by Hyun Suk's side, was wearing a slim black suit and skinny tie.

"The close family usually wears traditional clothes for special occasions," said Halmunee. "During those times, the men started wearing American-style suits instead of their hanboks."

Hyun Suk and Young Soo were clearly in love with each other. And now, Maya realized, they were also basking in the anxious joy of expectant parents.

It was so strange to think that her mother was in Hyun Suk's belly right now. That if she could place her hand on Hyun Suk's body, she might feel her mother's baby feet kick. The thought of that weirded Maya out.

"It was good because I ate a lot that day," said Halmunee. "I had the worst cravings for galbi jjim."

Maya's mouth watered at the thought of the tender and flavorful braised short ribs that were cooked so long they practically fell off the bone. The carrots, onions, and mushrooms that simmered along with the beef softened and darkened in the pot as they essentially became vehicles for the sauce. "Mmm. I used to love galbi jjim. But I haven't had that in forever."

Halmunee smiled. "I know. I'll show you how to make it soon. It's not that hard to cook. Just takes time."

"Yum," said Maya. "But why are we here this time? What did you want to show me?"

Halmunee shrugged. "I like parties. And I like cooking and eating miyeok-guk. You seemed to enjoy it too. And maybe you'll find something interesting. To draw, I mean."

She had that impish look on her face that Maya hated. It meant that she either was going to do something bad or was keeping secrets.

Maya knew there was no point in picking at her grandmother. The more she pressured Halmunee to tell her something, the tighter Halmunee clammed up. So instead Maya tried a different topic that she had been wanting to raise with her grandmother.

"Halmunee, do you have any food memories with my dad? Is there a way you could take me back so that I could see him when he was young?"

Halmunee's smile faded, and she looked at Maya for a long while before answering. "No. I can't take you back to see him. You need to have the right time."

"What's the right time?"

"Well, it's not now. Why are you wasting time here?" Halmunee nudged Maya forward. "We can talk later. Didn't you say you wanted to draw during our next trip? Well, this is it. So go and draw."

Maya could tell by the way Halmunee had her lips pressed together that there was no hope of getting any information out of her right now. It was infuriating trying to deal with her stubbornness.

But Halmunee was right. Maya had wanted to take this opportunity to draw their trips. There was so much to draw. She wanted to draw the towering pyramids of food lined up on the table, the people dressed in either traditional Korean clothes or mod outfits from the 1970s, and the decorations and banners that were draped around the room.

"How much time do we have left?" asked Maya.

"A few minutes or so," said Halmunee. "We should enjoy our-selves here for a bit. This was such a great party. Lots of good peo-ple, good food, and good drinks."

Maya eagerly scanned the room for a good vantage point. She wanted to capture these moments with pen and paper. She'd spent all her saved allowance money on sketchbooks with really nice thick paper that she put aside for these trips with Halmunee. In-stead of the doodles of animals, words, and unanswered questions that fit easily in her usual journal, these grand moments needed nicer, sturdier materials. There were so many people and details that Maya wanted to study later until they were stamped forever into her own memory.

"Is it okay if I walk around and explore?" Maya asked. "Will you be all right alone?"

If they had been at a real party, or any real event, Maya wouldn't have left Halmunee alone. But they were in the past and were invis-ible to everyone, so Maya didn't see the harm. Halmunee could run naked through the crowd, screaming at the top of her lungs, and it wouldn't make a single dent in the happiness of the people in the room.

Halmunee laughed. "Of course. Go, go. Have fun." She shooed Maya away. "But don't wander too far off. I'll find you when it's time."

"How?"

"You're the only one wearing shorts and sandals."

Maya looked down and smiled.

"Oh, right."

Halmunee was still sharp on her good days.

67

MIYEOK-GUK

By Halmunee, edited with specific measurements by Maya!

~~~~~~~~~

Dried seaweed (miyeok, ½ ounce)

Sesame oil (1 tbsp)

Beef (5 oz, chopped)

Onion (½ onion, sliced)

Garlic (1 tbsp, minced)

Korean soup soy sauce (gukganjang, 4 tbsp)

Water (5 cups, plus more for soaking seaweed)

Salt to taste

> Gukganjang is different from regular soy sauce and can be found in the Korean market. It's saltier, stronger flavored, and lighter in color. You can use regular soy sauce instead, but don't use too much. The soup will likely need more salt.

1. Soak the seaweed in cold water for 1 hour. Rinse, drain, and cut into finger-length pieces.

2. Pour the sesame oil into the bottom of a big pot.

3. Over medium-high heat, add the beef, onion, and garlic to the pot and stir until the beef is cooked.

4. Add the seaweed and several spoonfuls of soup soy sauce.

5. Stir until the seaweed is seasoned.

6. Add 5 cups of water and bring to a boil.

7. Boil over medium heat for 20 minutes, until seaweed is soft.

8. Taste and add salt if it's not salty enough.

9. Miyeok-guk is rich with nutrients. Serve for good health and on birthdays!

CHAPTER 8

PARTY CRASHER

Maya spent the next several minutes circling around the guests, trying to guess which were family and which were friends. Many of the guests had the trademark arched eyebrows and full lips of Halmunee's family.

The room was filling with the heat of the crowd, the aromas of the food on everyone's plates, and the pungent stink of smoke from the cigarettes dangling from almost every adult's hand. The flushed faces and increasingly loud voices hinted that people were enjoying plenty of alcohol, too. Even some of the teenagers were encouraged to sip soju, and their older relatives roared with laughter and clapped their backs when they coughed and sputtered from the fumes traveling down their throats and up their noses. This was the kind of party that no one wanted to leave and everyone would remember.

As Maya was making her way through the clusters of people and quickly sketching everyone she passed, a strange feeling made her stop. She scanned the crowd until she spotted the source: a stationary figure across the room was watching her. It was a boy, around Maya's age, maybe a little older, with floppy black hair that wasn't quite long enough to hide ears that stuck out a bit. His thick, straight eyebrows gave him a serious look that vanished when he saw her looking at him. With a slightly goofy grin, he held up his hand in a quick wave.

Maya looked behind her to see if there was someone else he could be waving to. There were several people behind her, but they were all from the past—unable to see her or, apparently, the boy.

Frowning, Maya weaved closer to him.

His stillness in the sea of people had first caught her eye, but then she noticed that, like her, he was dressed differently from the others in the crowd. Instead of traditional Korean or 1970s attire, he was wearing shorts, a Spinal Tap shirt that said THESE GO TO ELEVEN, and the whitest sneakers she'd ever seen.

It was clear that he could see Maya. How was that even possible?

If the boy had been David, or some other cute boy from school, she never would have had the courage to go up to him. But there was something a little dorky and approachable about this strange boy. And this wasn't exactly an ordinary situation.

Self-consciously crossing her arms across her middle, Maya nodded at him. "Hey."

He nodded back, still grinning. "Hi."

Like Mom, Maya wasn't one to stand around and make small talk as she slowly circled around the things she really wanted to talk about. Instead, she cut to the chase.

"So, you can see me?"

He paused for a second. Finally, he smiled. "I said hi to you, didn't

71

I? Why would I say hi to someone I couldn't see?"

Maya couldn't tell if he was being playful or making fun of her. Either way, it put her on the offensive. She didn't know what was happening to her, but lately her temper had been flaring up a lot more than usual. This often caused her to speak before she had a chance to think it over and soften the hard edges. Irritated, she cocked her head to the side.

"I hate it when people do that," she said. "Why can't you just answer my question normally instead of answering in a way that makes me feel stupid?"

His eyes went big and his eyebrows disappeared under his mop of hair. He held up his hands. "No, that wasn't what I meant."

Maya didn't let him continue. "I mean, you can't blame me for asking. I'm kind of new to this whole thing, but I at least know that no one here should be able to see me. Other than my grandmother, of course. So who are you, and why are you crashing my dimension?"

"I'm just here to enjoy a great party," he said, with a trace of a smile still on his face. "You know we can't actually eat anything here, but I've heard the food is fantastic. And how do you know you're not the one crashing my dimension?"

Maya paused. He had a point. She didn't know how Halmunee was doing this, so there was a small chance that they were crashing into the dimension of someone else at this party. She didn't know how to respond, so they continued staring at each other in silence, sizing each other up.

Finally, the boy took a deep breath and held out his hand. "Look, let's start over. Hi, I'm Jeff. I'm very good at putting my foot in my mouth when I'm trying to be funny."

Maya took his hand and shook it.

"Maya."

He paused, waiting for her to say something more. When it was clear she wasn't going to, he continued. "So, who's your halmunee?" he asked, his gaze traveling across the crowd.

He said only one Korean word, but Maya could already tell that his accent was much better than hers.

Concentrating on pronouncing the Korean words in her response carefully, she said, "Kim Hyun Suk. The young woman over there. And the old woman over there." She pointed out Halmunee, who was happily dancing by herself. "Where are you from?"

"Me? Oh, the DC area."

Maya had never traveled outside of California—other than these trips to Seoul with Halmunee, if you could count these as traveling. All she knew about DC was that it had a lot of monuments and museums. She would love being near so many museums.

"So how did you get here?" she asked.

"Same way as you, I imagine."

"But how?" asked Maya. "This can't be one of your memories. You're like my age."

"Yeah," said Jeff.

"But I'm from 2019."

"Yeah," said Jeff. "Same."

"So how are you here?" asked Maya.

"Because I'm special and awesome," said Jeff.

"No, really."

Jeff crossed his arms over his chest and rocked back on his heels, still smiling at her. "That's for me to know and for you to find out. But if you ask me nicely, maybe I'll tell you."

Maya rolled her eyes. She wondered if he was always this *on*, with all the constant joking and teasing. He was like a puppy, drawing your attention with his playfulness one second, and then the next second irritating you with his clawing and chewing. She imagined JEFF inscribed on a metal tag dangling from the collar of a hyperactive Golden Retriever puppy with large, floppy ears.

This was going to be as hard as trying to get information out of Halmunee.

"Fine. What's your secret . . . please?"

"That wasn't the nicest request I've ever gotten, but I guess that's the best I'll get out of you," said Jeff. "You're right. I am a party crasher. I can go to other times and places, even if they're not from my own memories. And I've met other people like us."

Maya gaped at him. "What? Who? And how?"

She hadn't thought such a thing was possible. Halmunee made it seem like this gift was only in their family. And she certainly didn't know how to do what Jeff did. Or did she? Was this yet another secret of Halmunee's she was holding back? And maybe if Jeff could teach her how to crash someone else's dimension, she could find a way to see her father—even without having any clear memories of him of her own.

But before Jeff could answer or Maya could ask more questions, Halmunee called out for her. "Maya, it's time!"

Halmunee was edging around the tables as she slowly made her way to Maya.

Maya swiveled back to Jeff.

"Looks like it's time for you to go," he said. "Don't worry. I'll find you the next time you visit. It'll be a nice day for a picnic."

"A picnic?" she echoed.

"Do you ever say anything other than repeating what I just said?" He laughed as he slowly walked backward into a crowd of guests.

As Halmunee wrapped her hand around Maya's wrist, she looked back at the younger versions of herself and Harabujee and said in a soft voice, "So much happiness here. One of the best moments of my life."

The last thing Maya saw before feeling that increasingly familiar tug back to the present was the flash of Jeff's smile and those ridiculous ears sticking out through his hair like the handles of a mug.

CHAPTER 9

NOT ABOUT A BOY

"Maya, what are you doing?"

Mom stuck her head out of the car window as she pulled into the garage.

Maya stopped rummaging through a dusty box, looked up at Mom, and sneezed.

"I was looking for some old photos of your family," said Maya. "For a project."

This wasn't necessarily a lie. It's just that it wasn't a school project she was working on; it was her own time-travel research. The birthday party trip had been only a few days ago and Maya wanted to match the faces she'd seen with any old photos she might find while everything was still fresh in her memory. But all she had found were her old baby toys, a bunch of outgrown clothes and shoes, and broken appliances.

"There's no point in digging through all this old stuff," said Mom. "We don't have any old family albums. They got ruined in the big flood."

Maya wondered what this flood was and when it happened. It couldn't have been at their current house, and they'd lived in this house for as long as she could remember. The way Mom said it made Maya picture a flood of biblical proportions, sweeping away hundreds of photos until they were sprinkled across the waves like confetti.

Despite what Mom said, Maya still held out hope that she could find something in the clutter. If Halmunee had managed to find that old wedding photo, maybe there were still some photos stuffed in a random box.

"But maybe there's some that were put in the wrong box somewhere and are still okay," said Maya with another sneeze.

"I'm sure that there's nothing there for you to find, and you're only making yourself dirty and aggravating your allergies," said Mom. "You know dust isn't good for you. Why don't you, me, and Halmunee take Gizmo to the dog park before the sun sets, and we can stop and get ice cream on the way back?"

"Okay!"

Maya shook off the dust that had settled on her and rushed inside to grab Gizmo. She wasn't finished looking, but that could wait. She couldn't say no to a trip to the dog park and ice cream.

The next day Jada stopped by Maya's house on the way to her violin lesson.

Maya had been lost in thought and only halfway listening to Jada go on about how great and funny Emma was, which then turned into her complaining about Izzy and their history collaboration.

"You missed another project meeting and Izzy couldn't stop freaking out."

"I did?"

"Yeah, what's going on with you lately?" Jada leaned across the countertop as Maya unloaded groceries from her afternoon trip to the Korean market.

Maya looked up quickly and smiled. "Nothing."

"Well, *something's* going on." Jada tapped her finger against her chin as she studied Maya. "I know it."

Jada had the unnerving skill of getting people to spill the latest gossip and share all sorts of secrets. She had a look that felt like she was piercing your soul. She said it was something she had learned from her mother, picked up after many years of confessing anytime she got in trouble.

Maya turned away and opened the refrigerator to put away the groceries, Gizmo faithfully at her feet.

Even with her back to her friend, Maya could feel Jada's eyes boring into the back of her skull with that infamous look Maya knew too well and had succumbed to way too often.

"Is this about your family thing you won't tell me about?" asked Jada, an edge of bitterness in her question.

"Kinda." Maya felt the uncomfortable tug-of-war between Friend Maya and Family Maya.

"Kinda? But it's not the only thing. Interesting." Jada smirked as she dug deeper. She either slowly picked away at the edges of the secret or lie until she got to the center of the truth, or she just took a sledgehammer and smashed her way through. Having been Maya's friend for so long, Jada knew that there was no point in using subtlety and immediately picked up the sledgehammer.

"This is about a boy, isn't it?"

Maya didn't answer.

"Then a girl?" asked Jada.

Maya opened the vegetable bin in the refrigerator and methodically unloaded the spinach and carrots. She had to nudge an eager Gizmo away from the carrots he loved so much.

"Not everything is about boys," she said to Jada.

"It is a boy! I knew it!" Jada raced to the refrigerator and leaned against it so that Maya couldn't avoid her piercing stare. "Spill! Who is it? Did something happen with David?"

"I told you already, it's not about a boy," Maya said as she fumbled with an empty grocery bag. She shut the refrigerator door and turned away, looking for something to do—anything to avoid Jada's relentless interrogation.

"Well, if you're not going to tell me what it is, I'm going to assume it's a boy. And I'm always right, so it's definitely about a boy."

Maya sighed and faced her friend. "Jay."

Jada tilted her head to the side and smiled. "My."

"You know it's almost three, right? Don't you have your violin lesson soon?"

Jada checked her phone and yelped. Dashing across the kitchen, she pointed back at Maya. "We are not done with this conversation. To be continued!"

Maya watched Jada disappear out the door. She wanted so badly to tell Jada about Halmunee and Jeff. To tell her everything. Jada was her best friend and knew almost everything there was to know about her, but this was one secret Maya couldn't let go. Not yet.

How could she? How could she explain the impossible to her friend without showing her some kind of proof, without yet understanding it herself?

Maya had tried asking Halmunee if she could bring others with them on their trips, but Halmunee shut that down immediately. A twinge of guilt prevented Maya from saying anything more. She didn't want Halmunee to think that she was trying to ditch her grandmother to hang out with her friends.

Maya knew that Halmunee had been burned before by telling her secret to her cousin. But maybe if she could show all this to Jada firsthand, her best friend would believe her. It wouldn't be like what went down between Halmunee and Soon Mi. Jada had always been loving and supportive of Maya in all their years of friendship.

Distracted by these thoughts, Maya munched on a handful of wasabi peas, the only decent snack Mom regularly kept stocked in the house.

"Maya?" Halmunee, groggy and disoriented, shuffled into the kitchen.

Maya's hopes sank. If Halmunee was already off to a rough start, this wasn't likely to be a good day.

"How are you feeling?"

Maya quickly switched from Friend Maya to Family Maya and helped Halmunee sit down on the stool that was just vacated by Jada. Maybe if Halmunee had some time to sit quietly and fully wake up, she would perk up a bit.

"I'm fine," said Halmunee. She patted Maya's hand, her favorite method of showing affection for her granddaughter. She looked at the open bag of wasabi peas on the countertop. "Did you eat yet?

You can't make a full meal out of those."

"I was waiting for you," said Maya. "I was thinking we could make something together. Maybe something you'd make for a picnic? But if you're feeling tired, I can just make us some sandwiches."

Halmunee's face lit up and her fatigue seemed to disappear. She clapped her hands excitedly. "Oh, a picnic! What a good idea. We can make gimbap. It's the perfect food for a picnic, and everyone should know how to make gimbap. I can't believe your omma or halmunee didn't teach you before."

Maya hesitated. Halmunee had forgotten who Maya was again. This wasn't a good sign.

She debated whether to stop Halmunee and try making gimbap another time, but she wanted so badly to go to whatever picnic Halmunee had in mind and possibly run into Jeff again.

She couldn't rely on Halmunee to answer all of her questions. Halmunee had already proven herself adept at holding back secrets. Not even Jada would be able to unravel the truth from Halmunee's silences and mixed-up memories. But Maya had to at least try.

Halmunee was only going to get worse over time. Who knew when they'd have another opportunity to do this?

And Maya couldn't wait any longer.

CHAPTER 10

PYRAMID OF GIMBAPS

Maya's guilt faded away as she watched Halmunee bustling around the kitchen, perking up a bit and looking more alert. Maybe the act of remembering the recipe and making the gimbap would help clear the fog clouding Halmunee's mind that afternoon.

"Now we get everything ready," said Halmunee. "Where's the kogi?"

She rummaged in the freezer and cried out in triumph as she pulled out a medium-sized portion of beef. "Aha! Always keep some in the back, just in case."

As the meat thawed in a large bowl of water in the sink, Halmunee seasoned and prepared the spinach and thinly sliced carrots, while Maya followed instructions to add salt and sesame oil to the rice and mixed it all together. Sesame oil made everything smell and taste better.

Maya was growing hungry and she nibbled on the pickled radishes, savoring the sour, vinegary flavor that woke up her taste buds and had them demanding more.

Halmunee slapped Maya's hand away from a third piece. "Stop eating all the takuan. You'll spoil your appetite. And we need those. Go and cook the eggs."

Maya shrugged and took several eggs out of the refrigerator. "No problem. I can do that."

Just as she was about to crack the eggs into the pan, Halmunee stopped her and pushed a bowl into her hands.

"No, no, no. Stir them in here first with a pinch of salt and then pour into the pan. And don't scramble them. They should be cooked thin, like an omelet."

"Okay," said Maya.

There was something comforting about cooking with Halmunee. The gentle *thunk*s of the knife hitting the cutting board, the aromas wrapping around them, and the occasional bumping against each other as they reached for a bowl or ingredient made the kitchen feel more alive and more like home than any other room in the house. It used to be a sterile, boring room that Maya only visited to grab something quick to eat from the refrigerator or to wash her dirty plates and cups, but was now a place that bubbled with energy and brightness.

One after another, Maya cracked the eggs into the bowl. With a fork, she broke the bright yellow yolks and stirred to blend them with the whites before adding some salt. Then she poured the contents into the greased pan. The eggs raced to the edges, gurgling with the heat. There was nothing better than the smells and sounds of an egg frying in a buttered pan.

She started to lift up the edges to fold it over when Halmunee stopped her.

"No, no, no." That was starting to become a catchphrase for Halmunee. "The eggs should be *like* an omelet, but not an omelet."

"You didn't say that before," Maya said before she could stop herself. "You said 'like an omelet.' And that was it."

"I think I know what I said," snapped Halmunee.

Maya stopped and took a deep breath. Halmunee had been getting better as they worked in the kitchen, but setbacks could happen at any point. Maya had almost forgotten about Halmunee's condition and was arguing back like she would have done with Jada or Mom. But she couldn't afford to do that with Halmunee and potentially aggravate her.

Halmunee continued, her voice evening out as she spoke, "Don't you remember? Keep it flat and then turn off the heat. When it cools, cut it into wide strips, like the takuan there, and put them on the plate."

Maya did just that, silently and obediently, while Halmunee, with the skillful hand of an experienced chef, cooked up the beef that she had cut into small pieces and marinated.

Maya still hadn't said anything to Mom about how Halmunee had used the stove on her own to make doenjang jjigae. She meant to, but Halmunee hadn't done it again. Maya was always with her when she cooked now. And so Maya purposely kept forgetting to bring it up.

Halmunee's mood lightened as she finished with the beef and spooned it into a bowl.

"Now, let's roll," said Halmunee, giggling at her own joke. Any trace of her earlier temper was gone.

Smiling with relief at the return of the calm energy radiating through the kitchen, Maya asked, "What can I do to help?"

"Watch me first, and then you can try later. And you can take care of the ends."

Halmunee laid flat a large piece of gim on a mat made of thin stalks of bamboo, a smaller version of the mat Maya liked to lie on to keep cool. This single sheet of dried seaweed was the wrap that would hold everything together. Next, she spread a thin layer of the seasoned rice over the gim, patting it down with the rice scooper to even it out. Then, using a pair of chopsticks, she laid all the ingredients lengthwise along the center of the rice.

Maya mentally double-checked to make sure that nothing was forgotten. And then Halmunee worked her magic with the bamboo mat and put everything together to make gimbap.

Lifting up the gim and the rice by rolling the mat over the fillings, Halmunee squeezed firmly and continued rolling, inching the mat more and more until it revealed a long and tight roll. The shiny black gim fully encased the rice and fillings, except for the small bits that stuck out at the ends.

Halmunee wiped a small amount of sesame oil on a large sharp knife.

"Makes it easier to cut," she explained to Maya. "So the knife doesn't stick to the rice and gim."

With swift and decisive movements, Halmunee sliced up the roll and arranged the cut pieces on a clean plate in concentric circles. Maya was happy to discover that "taking care of the ends" meant eating the messy pieces Halmunee chopped off the ends of the rolls.

She was excellent at that job.

Halmunee repeated the process several more times, cutting and placing the gimbap so that soon there was a pyramid stacked high on the plate.

"Now you try," said Halmunee.

Maya was eager to take Halmunee's place. She'd never really cooked or baked much before, but there was something about the methodical process that magically transformed a plate of ingredients into a disc of goodness that appealed to her. And Halmunee made it look so easy.

Maya took her time putting together her first gimbap roll. When she finished squeezing the bamboo mat to reveal a perfectly shaped roll, she was so pleased she was practically beaming, as if she were a proud mother of a gimbap baby.

"I did it!"

Halmunee smiled and nodded. "Good, good. Now cut it up and I'll get a new plate. When making gimbap, it's always good to make a lot. They go so quickly."

Maya struggled a bit to cut her roll into clean pieces. The knife kept sticking to the rice and gim and pulling it apart. Her pieces weren't perfect, but they still looked pretty good. She put aside the end pieces for Halmunee. It was only fair. After stacking her pieces, she made another roll, and another roll after that, each time getting better.

When Maya had made a tall pyramid of gimbaps on her own plate, Halmunee reached out and stopped Maya's hands from reaching for another piece of gim.

"Are you ready?" Halmunee said.

Maya tilted her head and looked at Halmunee quizzically. She had been so caught up in the process of making gimbap and enjoying her time with her grandmother, she'd almost forgotten about her original goal of getting to a picnic. With a small jump, Maya moved closer to Halmunee.

"Oh, yes!"

After wiping her hands on a dishtowel, Maya hoisted a small bag that held a pocket sketchbook and drawing supplies onto her shoulder. She reached out and held Halmunee's hand. Smiling at each other, they each picked up a couple pieces of gimbap.

"All in one bite," said Halmunee. "It's best when you stuff it in so all the flavors mix together." She shoved one piece completely into her mouth, her cheeks bulging as she chewed.

Maya did the same. As her teeth sank into the gimbap and the tightly wrapped roll of flavors unraveled in her mouth, she felt herself being pulled back, far away from the sleek black pyramids sitting on the counter.

CHAPTER 11

LEAVING THE PICNIC

The sunlight was so dazzling, it took a few blinks before Maya's vision cleared and she could see where—and when—they'd arrived.

They had landed in a wide, open meadow bordered by trees. Several groups of young girls, dressed in school uniforms of crisp white shirts and long dark skirts, were setting up picnic blankets across the lush grass. A simple red gate, with two pillars and a spiked top, stood in the distance. A straight stone-covered path led from the gate to a small red and green wooden building. And behind the building rose a large green hill with a flattened top where another smaller mound stood, surrounded by stone statues. The grassy hills were too smooth and symmetrical to be natural.

Maya turned to Halmunee and pointed at the hills. "What are those?"

"They're . . . they're . . ." Halmunee paused as she tried to find the word. Maya wasn't sure if Halmunee had forgotten the word or if she was just stuck trying to think of the appropriate translation. Like Mom, Halmunee spoke fluent English, but sometimes an uncommonly used word or idiom would throw her off. Finally Halmunee landed on a word, though she didn't seem satisfied with it. "Graves?"

"Graves?" Maya looked down and then scanned the grassy expanse for any sign of tombstone markers.

Halmunee shook her head. "No. That's not right. Not quite graves. What is it called where they bury kings and queens?"

Maya thought to herself before tentatively suggesting, "Tombs?"

Halmunee's face lit up. "Yes, that's it! That's an ancient royal tomb. Where they buried the king. There are others here, too."

"You went on picnics at tombs?" Maya thought that seemed a little morbid and found the contrast between the laughing girls and the solemn location slightly disturbing.

"Why is that weird?" asked Halmunee. "It's educational and fun. How is it any different than the field trips you took to museums with mummies?"

She had a point.

"So, this was a field trip? How far from Seoul are we?"

"We're in Seoul. The rest of the city is just beyond the trees. Isn't it peaceful here? You'd never know we were right in the middle of the city."

"Wow." Maya was starting to see the appeal of this place. It wasn't as if they were in a creepy cemetery filled with graves. It was more like a sacred park. She wondered if Mom and Dad had gone on similar trips, since they both had grown up in Seoul too.

She turned back to the cheerful groups of girls and moved closer to them, but jumped when Halmunee cried out, "Don't do that!"

Maya stepped back. "What? What's wrong? Are you okay?"

Halmunee pulled Maya closer to her. "I'm fine. You just shouldn't walk on that path."

Maya looked at the stone path she had innocently stepped on. Nothing appeared wrong with it, other than that it was slightly uneven, with one side higher than the other. But Halmunee's sharp tone and pinched expression spoke of more than just a worry that Maya might trip.

"Why? What's wrong with it?"

"Stay on the lower path, to the left," said Halmunee. "The one you were standing on before, that's meant for spirits. That's the path for the dead king. We're not ghosts yet. We've had to deal with enough death in our past. No point in tempting it to come back for us."

"Let's go closer to the picnic then," Maya said, looping her arm through Halmunee's. She was determined to move forward and not let herself or Halmunee get bogged down with dark thoughts. She nodded toward the picnicking girls and asked, "Which one are you?"

The girls were all dressed alike and had similar bobbed hair. Maya wasn't sure if she'd be able to find the younger version of her grandmother on her own.

Halmunee pointed to the largest and loudest group in the choice area partially shaded by a cluster of trees. One of the girls seemed to be putting on a one-woman show, and the others were clapping and shouting in approval. Maya had a bit of a hard time keeping up with the rapid-fire delivery and dated slang from afar, but her Korean comprehension was good enough that she got the gist of the story. Something about a dog chasing a chicken and making someone fall on their butt.

Joining the group, Halmunee sat and laughed along with the other girls. At first, Maya thought that Halmunee was sitting next to the younger version of herself. But as Maya's gaze traveled across the group, she found herself repeatedly drawn to the girl standing and engaging her friends. When the girl gave a dramatic end to her story and finished with an impish grin, Maya immediately recognized her.

So that was Hyun Suk.

Hyun Suk was even younger here than on the doenjang jjigae trip when Maya had seen her as a teenager. Here, she was a couple years younger than Maya and she bounced and smiled with a lightness that had been absent in that other memory. Maya was drawn by the magnetic force of Hyun Suk's energy and had started to move to join the group when something caught her eye. Someone was waving at her from behind one of the trees.

Jeff.

Maya looked back at Halmunee and motioned that she was leaving the picnic to explore and draw. Halmunee nodded and turned back to her past, while Maya tripped over a clump of grass as she headed toward Jeff.

CHAPTER 12

DISCOVERING NEW THINGS

"You made it," said Jeff, a wide smile on his face.

He was wearing almost the exact same outfit as before, and Maya was tempted to tease him about his huge white sneakers.

"Of course I did," said Maya. "Why wouldn't I?"

"I don't know. Maybe you broke your flux capacitor or something . . ."

Jeff grinned and looked at Maya, waiting for her to react.

"Come on," said Jeff. "Not even a single laugh?"

"What do you mean?"

"What do I mean? Doc! The DeLorean! *Back to the Future*!"

Maya frowned. "Oh, from that old movie? I've never seen it."

Jeff raised a hand to his chest and stumbled back dramatically. "Never seen it? It's only the greatest movie ever made. I can't believe you've never seen it!"

"Nope."

While Jeff continued his dramatics, Maya decided it was time to steer things onto the right track.

"So. Your secret."

Jeff straightened up and smoothed his ruffled hair. "Fine. But you have to promise me that you'll watch *Back to the Future*."

"Deal. Now, tell me your secret!"

"How much have you been told about all this?" Jeff asked, gesturing around the park. "What do you know so far?"

"I know that we've been traveling back to the past, but we aren't really a part of the past. My halmunee explained it's like each moment is a movie and we're traveling through a multiscreen theater watching different movies, different moments from her past."

Jeff nodded. "Okay. That's actually not a bad way to put it. So, let's stick with that analogy then." He stretched his arms out. "This moment that you've traveled to, this picnic, is a movie. Let's say it's a two p.m. showing of *Back to the Future*. Or more like *Back to the Past*."

Maya snorted at Jeff's joke.

"Now, that's easy enough to get. But think of this. How many times do you think your halmunee has been at this moment? The older she gets, the more she might want to revisit some of her favorite memories. Say she's seen this moment—this movie—three times. Well, why haven't you seen other versions of her here, revisiting this one moment in time? Why aren't the other versions of your halmunee in the audience with us?"

Maya hadn't thought about that. Of course Halmunee must have visited this scene many times. The same with the birthday celebration and the patbingsu afternoon. Each of those trips had been to one, discrete moment in time. So each time Halmunee went back, it had to be to that same one moment, right? But each visit, they had been the only ones there in that time-traveling dimension; they hadn't met up with three other ghostly Halmunees of various ages who were also dipping back in time.

Jeff's eyes lit up and he continued talking in earnest.

He'd make a good teacher, Maya thought. He had the natural talent and passion that made people get excited and want to learn more.

"The reason you don't see other versions of your halmunee or yourself is because each time you come back, you enter a slightly different dimension, and these dimensions don't interact with each other. It's like, say twenty-year-old Halmunee and fifty-year-old Halmunee are both seeing a five p.m. showing of this moment. But there are two rooms for this showing. So twenty-year-old Halmunee is in room one and fifty-year-old Halmunee is in the next one, room two. Each of the times she's visited this moment, she's been in a different dimension, a different room. They all exist together—different rooms in this one movie theater. Get it?"

"I think so." Maya nodded slowly. "But what about the others? You said there were others like us, right?"

"Oh, yeah," said Jeff enthusiastically. "Think about it. What are the odds that you and your halmunee are the only ones who can do this? There are others who have this ability to travel back. The same rules apply to their visits. They each have their own movie theater and their own films to watch. Sometimes there's a movie that's playing in multiple theaters, an overlap of a moment with multiple travelers. All these different dimensions, or movie theaters, are why you don't see anyone else who's traveling back. They can't interact with the past or the other dimensions and the people traveling in them."

"But how does that explain you?" asked Maya. "How are you here?"

"Like I said the first time we met, how do you know that you're not in my movie theater?" Jeff smirked at her. "So rude, storming into it, uninvited, and with no ticket."

Maya grinned. "I am here as a guest of my halmunee, and she would never do anything rude like that. You, on the other hand, seem exactly that rude. And besides, I don't even know how to travel on my own, let alone cross into your dimension."

"No," said Jeff, turning serious again. "You can do it too."

"But I can't. I've never gone back by myself. These are my halmunee's memories. Not mine."

"You will." Jeff said it so confidently, Maya almost believed him. "You have it in you. Otherwise you wouldn't be able to walk around separately from your halmunee. Visitors usually have to maintain constant physical contact with the traveler."

"Visitors?" Maya leaned in eagerly. "So, I can bring people back with me so long as we stay together? Anyone?"

Before Jeff could answer, Maya heard Halmunee weakly calling for her. "Maya! Where are you? It's time!"

Halmunee sounded tired. These trips always seemed to take a lot out of her.

"I have to go," said Maya, pulling away yet reluctant to leave.

"Keep practicing," said Jeff. "Not just with your halmunee. Try it on your own, with your own memories. And when you do it, concentrate on that moment in the past. Imagine yourself there. Focus on the smallest details you can. And the stronger the emotion or connection to the food, the easier it will be. You can do it. I know you can. And if you ever get lost or need me, just come back here and give me a shout. I'll find you eventually."

"How?" asked Maya

"We've created a connection between our two movie theaters now," said Jeff. "It's like our movie theaters are next door to each other and I can go to my theater or yours to watch the same movie as you."

"Maya!" Halmunee called out again.

"Why not give me your number and we can talk in real time?" asked Maya.

"That's not as much fun." Jeff gave her a mock salute goodbye. "I'll see you soon."

Maya turned away, tracing her path back to the picnic. She tried resisting the urge to look over her shoulder but didn't succeed. Jeff was watching her and frowning, his brows drawn together and a slight crease forming between them. When he saw her looking back, he gave her a lopsided grin and waved with both hands over his head.

"Oh, and next time you travel with your halmunee to a different moment, wear something red," he said.

"Red?"

"Yeah!"

"Um, okay."

Maya turned and ran back to Halmunee.

"Where were you?" asked Halmunee, grabbing Maya's arm as she emerged from the grouping of trees.

Halmunee looked pale and tired. She leaned heavily on Maya's arm and walked so slowly Maya had to consciously curb her normal pace.

Maya hesitated. She felt the familiar clash between Family Maya and Friend Maya.

She wanted to keep Jeff to herself for now. When had she become so secretive? She wasn't sure how she felt about this change, but still she decided to keep him to herself for the moment.

"Oh, I was just hanging around." She waved her hand casually back toward the trees. "You know, discovering new things."

CHAPTER 13

RED RED

It was getting harder and harder to practice with Halmunee as her bad days started to outnumber the good. She was more easily irritated, and there were times when Maya could see where Mom got her temper from. She talked fondly of her life in Korea, but her memories were scrambled and she often didn't remember where she was or who Maya was. Maya was torn between wanting to continue to practice and wanting to make sure she didn't tire out Halmunee. The strain of the trips to the past seemed like it would be too much for her.

One night on their way to bed, Maya and Mom caught Halmunee about to head outside in her pajamas.

"Where are you going?" asked Mom.

"To the market," said Halmunee. "I need green onions so I can finish making lunch."

Gently, Mom guided Halmunee back up the stairs.

"It's okay," said Mom. "I'll get them. Maya, why don't you make some tea and bring it up for Halmunee?"

As Maya boiled water for Halmunee's tea, she felt even more determined to learn how to travel back on her own. If she could just learn how to do it herself, maybe she could carry the brunt of the burden so that Halmunee could relax and enjoy reliving the favorite memories she had shared with Maya. And maybe she could convince Halmunee to relive some past moments that involved Dad so that Maya could get to know him. It would be even better than dragging out the tiny pieces of information from Mom, bit by bit, or hoping to find old faded photos.

Sometimes, unexpectedly, Halmunee would have a good day and be full of energy and wit. As soon as Mom left to run some errands on one of the good days, Halmunee told Maya that it was time to make some bindaetteok.

"What are those?" asked Maya.

"Chop up those green onions and kimchi, and I'll show you," said Halmunee.

As Maya chopped up the ingredients, her fingertips turned bright red from the kimchi. After Halmunee smashed some mung beans that had been soaking overnight, she added garlic, soy sauce, sesame oil, and salt. Next, she directed Maya to add the green onions and kimchi into the mixture. Maya didn't think the mixture looked all that appetizing so far, but the aroma of the garlic and sesame oil made up for its appearance. And she knew that she could trust Halmunee with making something delicious from the library of Korean recipes in her head . . . for now.

Maya had taken to writing down how to make Halmunee's traditional dishes. She illustrated them with the different ingredients in one of her new sketchbooks. She tried her best to estimate amounts, since Halmunee never measured anything. Anytime she asked Halmunee how much of a certain ingredient she should add, Halmunee would just say, "What looks right" or "Until it tastes good."

Halmunee fried the ingredients into pancakes three at a time in a large skillet. As the pancakes turned golden brown and Halmunee flipped them, their aroma wafted through the kitchen and made Maya's mouth water. While they waited, Halmunee quickly put together some soy-and-vinegar dipping sauce in a small bowl. When the pancakes were crisp along the edges, she slid each one off the spatula and onto the plate.

"Go ahead," she said. "They taste best when they're still hot!"

Too eager to deal with chopsticks, Maya picked up her first bindaetteok with her hands, blowing on the piping-hot pancake as her fingers danced along the edge searching for a cool spot. A quick dunk in the dipping sauce was all that was needed to complete the hearty and satisfying snack. As the sauce traveled up through the bindaetteok, it spread its salty and sour flavors throughout the savory pancake.

"Okay," said Halmunee. "Ready?"

Just as Halmunee grabbed hold of her, Maya snatched up her bag that held her sketchbook, art supplies, and a red sweater. She had been keeping it in the kitchen just in case Halmunee took her on another surprise trip.

They were back at the house where the doenjang jjigae had taken them. Maya peeked into the house and saw the teenage version of

Halmunee cooking bindaetteok with her mother.

"My omma used to always cook a lot of bindaetteok on the first day of school," Halmunee said softly. "She knew they were my favorite."

As Halmunee walked into the house, Maya asked, "Is it okay if I take a look around? I didn't get much of a chance during the jjigae visit, and I want to draw the house from a distance."

"Yes," said Halmunee. "I'll find you when it's time to go."

So Maya left to find Jeff, while Halmunee watched her younger self cook bindaetteok with her mother.

Maya wasn't exactly sure how Jeff was going to find her, but she pulled on the red sweater she'd borrowed from Jada. She normally didn't like wearing such bright colors and had a closet filled with muted shades of blue and green, but she figured the more noticeable the sweater was, the better.

"Maya?"

"Jeff?"

Jeff appeared from behind a tree.

"I said red, but I didn't mean red red."

Maya folded her arms across her chest in irritation. "You said red; I'm wearing red. Better than what you're wearing."

She eyed his ridiculously short running shorts.

Jeff grinned. "What are you talking about? I look fresh, and you know it. You're looking at the number one long-distance runner in my school district. I even ran a half marathon once. I would have won my age bracket if I hadn't hurt my knee."

Maya snorted. "Sure. Whatever you say." She peered back at Halmunee and then turned to Jeff. "So, can we get started now? I still have so many more questions."

"Don't worry about it," said Jeff. "Time is relative."

"Okay, Professor Jeff. But really, I don't want my halmunee forgetting about me and leaving on her own."

"Don't worry. We won't be gone long. We just need to find some time to hang out in." Jeff held out his hand to her. "I don't want to freak you out, but this is going to seem really weird to you at first. Now, don't say anything. I need to concentrate. And whatever you do, don't let go."

Maya tried to subtly wipe her hand on her sweater before grabbing his hand.

"Ready?"

Unsure of whether she could trust her voice to hide her nervousness, she looked up at him and nodded.

Jeff closed his eyes and stood so still Maya could barely even see him breathing. His hand held hers, cold and unmoving. It was so quiet that when he finally gasped, she jumped.

His eyes were open, but they seemed unfocused. There was a peaceful but dazed expression on his face.

"Hold on . . ." Jeff's voice sounded strange and far off, as if he was already somewhere else and was calling to her from there.

He squeezed her hand so tight she could feel their pulses, synced to the same rhythm. Dragging her alongside him, he took one large step forward and the world fell apart around Maya.

This wasn't like her trips back with Halmunee. At least with those there was some sense of linear movement. They were moving either forward or back. There were always sights, sounds, and smells that flooded her senses.

There was none of that this time. With nothing to fixate on, she couldn't tell if she was right side up or upside down; if she was seeing everything or nothing. They could have been floating in this void for a second or several years. The only thing that was familiar to Maya was the steady pressure on her hand and their two heartbeats pounding together.

BINDAETTEOK

By Halmunee, edited with specific measurements by Maya!

~~~~~~~

Dried mung beans (2 cups)

Water (¾–1 cup, plus more for soaking)

Salt (½ tsp)

Soy sauce (2 tsp)

Garlic (1 tsp minced)

Sesame oil (1 tbsp)

Additional ingredients as desired: green onions, kimchi, mung bean sprouts, and/or chopped meat or seafood

Vegetable oil for frying

DIPPING SAUCE

2 tbsp soy sauce

1 tbsp rice vinegar

Gochugaru (red pepper flakes) to taste

1. Rinse the dried mung beans and soak in water for 5–6 hours until soft. Drain.

2. Blend the mung beans with the water and salt.

3. Combine the mung beans with the soy sauce, garlic, and sesame oil.

4. Add whatever additional ingredients you want to use, such as sliced green onions, mung bean sprouts, chopped kimchi (1 cup), and/or chopped meat or seafood.

5. Heat a little bit of vegetable oil in a pan over medium heat.

6. Pour some of the batter onto the pan in the form of a pancake.

7. Cook until the batter is golden brown.

8. Flip pancake and cook for a couple more minutes until golden brown on both sides and slightly crisp along the edges.

9. Repeat with the rest of the batter.

10. For dipping sauce, mix together soy sauce and rice vinegar. Add some gochugaru (red pepper flakes) for an extra kick of spice.

11. Eat while hot, with dipping sauce!

CHAPTER 14

JEWELED MEMORIES

A slight tug pulled Maya out of the nothingness. Her toe caught on something and she fell forward, pulling Jeff down with her.

"You okay?" Jeff asked, helping her up.

"Yeah." Maya's voice was hoarse and shaky. "What was that? Where are we? Or wait, also, when are we?"

They were in almost complete darkness. Maya squeezed Jeff's hand tightly so that they wouldn't lose each other.

"It's okay." Jeff sounded extra loud in the middle of this black emptiness. "Turn around."

"Don't let go!" Maya shouted.

"I won't. Don't worry, I still have you. Just turn slowly around with me."

Maya felt herself guided into a circle until she saw a dim light glowing in the distance.

"Using your halmunee's analogy, you could say that we're at the mother of all movie theaters. Come on, I'll show you."

Together, they ran toward the light. They were racing so fast it felt like they were flying to the sun. As they neared the source of the illumination, Maya saw that it wasn't a single light, but many. Hundreds, thousands, maybe millions.

"Oh," Maya whispered. "They're trees."

A dazzling orchard stood in the middle of this endless darkness. Each tree seemed illuminated from within like a pumpkin carved up and lit on Halloween.

Maya's heart raced, not just from their run but from excitement at this unreal sight.

They stopped in front of a simple wooden gate in a fence that seemed to stretch forever in both directions. Behind the gate stood an enormous orchard of giant brilliant trees. Maya reached out to open the gate, but Jeff pulled her back.

"We need to ask for permission first," said Jeff.

Confused, Maya watched as Jeff tapped on the gate. The wooden beams shook in their posts and, to her surprise, the vibrations released a soft song, like chimes but lower and deeper. As the music faded, the gate slowly swung open.

As Maya crossed the threshold, she looked down at the maze of thick roots that crawled across the ground; they must have been the bumps she'd tripped over earlier. The ground fell and rose in grassy peaks amid a heavy fog that gave the illusion that they were high up in the mountains. Flitting her gaze back and forth from the ground to the trees arching over them, trying to take in everything at once, she carefully stepped around the roots and followed after Jeff.

Once they were among the trees, Maya tilted her head back to gaze at the lit-up branches and leaves above them. An occasional bright leaf flitted across the treetops in the endless black sky. The branches and leaves glowed with the same light as the tree trunks, but what really took Maya's breath away was the dazzling jeweled orbs strung throughout the trees.

Jeff stopped in front of one of the trees and turned to Maya.

"What do you think of the orchard?"

"It's the most beautiful thing I've ever seen," Maya said. "Those jewels look almost like persimmons up in the branches."

Maya pointed up at one of the jewels that was the same brilliantly vivid orange as the persimmons Mom often peeled and cut for her as a snack. She marveled at how similar they looked to persimmons, from their squat round shape to the trademark symmetrical and delicate four leaves at the top.

"Huh," said Jeff. "They look like persimmons to you? That's interesting. To me they look like peaches. I think everyone sees them differently."

"But what are they?" asked Maya.

Jeff patted the tree trunk next to him. "See for yourself. Take a look at one of them."

A branch moved down toward Maya until a persimmon that dangled from a dainty stem at the end was just above her head. She stood on her tiptoes and peered closer. At first, all she could see was her own reflection on the facets of the jewel. Tentatively, she reached out and touched it with her fingertips. At her touch, light spilled out from the fruit and smoke swirled within it, sweeping away her reflection. She squinted at the scene emerging from the smoke as though she were peering out an opaque window on a foggy morning.

Inside the persimmon, a small version of herself and Jada on the first day of kindergarten emerged. Little Maya fiddled with the hem of her crisp new dress, looking around for someone to talk to or something to do. She meandered to the sprawling jungle gym in the middle of the playground. From the very top of the jungle gym, Jada dangled upside down, her braids swaying in the wind. Jada waved and called out to little Maya, "Want to play?" A smile broke out across little Maya's relieved face and she climbed up to meet Jada. And just like that, they were new best friends.

Smoke swirled inside the persimmon and quickly solidified as soon as the scene was over. In a few seconds, Maya's fingers were once again resting on a persimmon that showed nothing more than her own reflection. As quickly as the scene had first appeared, it dissolved and was swallowed up by the smoke. The light pulled back until it once again rested completely within the persimmon. She let go of it and the branch moved away from her.

Feeling a little dazed, Maya stepped back and rubbed her eyes.

"Are you okay?" he asked. "What did you see?"

"I saw me on my first day of kindergarten." Maya looked at Jeff. "What's in these?"

"This is life," said Jeff. "This is time." He reached out to a persimmon and light shone from it. "This is the time you went to the beach with your mother and got stung by a jellyfish." He reached out to another persimmon. "And this is the time you fought with your mother and ran away from home and hid in the treehouse of your friend Jada. You were so mad. And your mom was so scared."

Maya had almost forgotten about that time she ran away. It had been years ago. Although now that she thought back to that moment, Mom hadn't seemed scared at all. She'd been so mad when Jada's parents had brought her back home, she grounded Maya for the rest of that summer.

"I don't understand," said Maya. "Why does this tree have all my memories?"

Jeff let go of the persimmon in his hand, and with a soft shushing of leaves the branches lifted skyward, taking their jewels back out of reach. "Oops, sorry. I forgot how strange it can be. This place isn't just about you. And it's not really about memories. This place is time itself."

Maya stared at Jeff. "What do you mean?"

"Each tree is the timeline of a single person. Past, present, future. Some trees interact with others, crossing branches and roots, and maybe even with their jewels.

"Think of each tree as the movie theater from your halmunee's analogy," Jeff continued. "And each of these persimmons on your movie-theater tree is a movie moment of your life."

Maya gazed in wonder at the endless canopy of glowing branches and fluttering leaves dancing among them.

"How many trees are there?" she asked.

Jeff looked around the orchard and shrugged. "Oh, that's impossible to know. There's no real number. I guess it's like an infinite number of trees."

Maya reached out and touched the tree trunk that held all the moments of her life. A jolt went through her arm and then her entire body.

The bark was rough and sharp in places where it twisted and bent.

Looking up, she could see the tiny glittering jewels of her persimmons high above among the dancing leaves.

"So, you can find out everything there is to know about me?" she asked. "About my family? About my future?"

"Theoretically, yes," said Jeff. "Well, kind of. But the tree won't let anyone, not even you, see your future. Doing that can really mess things up in time. There are some things you're meant to know now, and there are some things you're meant to know tomorrow."

Maya's thoughts immediately jumped to the big hole from her past that continued to haunt her present.

"What about my dad?"

CHAPTER 15

JEFF'S SECRET

Maya knew that seeing Dad's tree wouldn't be quite the same as really meeting him. She wouldn't be able to touch him or talk to him. He would never be able to get to know her and understand the type of person his daughter had grown up to be. He wouldn't even be able to see her. But she could learn about him. She could get to know him in a way that would at least partially fill the void in her world, and maybe get some answers to the questions her mom ignored.

She eagerly scanned the orchard, peering through the fog, hoping to see a tree that felt right. She was certain she'd know her father's tree.

Jeff shook his head. "I'm sorry. I don't know which tree is his so it would be a process of elimination to go through the orchard. I'm limited in what I can do."

Maya felt deflated. If she knew which tree was his, she could get to know her dad. She wouldn't have to rely on the hope that she might get to visit one of the few memories Halmunee might have with him and Mom.

But before she could wallow deeper into disappointment, she remembered another question.

"Wait, speaking of what you do . . . how do you travel?"

"Food. It's the same as with you and your halmunee. When you travel back with your halmunee, you get pulled back to a specific moment that your halmunee remembers related to the food she's eating, right? Well, I do the same with memories that are tied to certain foods I've eaten. As soon as I smell and taste a certain food, I just disappear into my memories."

"Really?" asked Maya. "Like what? What was your first time?"

Biting his lip, Jeff hesitated before answering.

"Well, my first time was when I was out eating pizza with my friends and my parents came to get me to tell me that my brother had been hit by a car while riding his bike."

Maya didn't know what to say. Death had shaped her family, too—her father, her grandfather. She knew about the emptiness that it left behind.

"Oh, Jeff. I'm so sorry."

"Thanks." Jeff turned slightly away from Maya and cleared his throat. "We were really close. Closer than either of us were to my older brother. Michael was only a year younger than me. And so when he died, I was so . . . so . . . angry. It wasn't fair. He was only *eleven*," Jeff said, his voice growing louder. "He was the smartest, the nicest, the funniest of us all."

He stopped and took a deep breath before continuing more quietly. "While my parents were busy preparing for Michael's funeral, we ordered takeout a lot since none of us felt like cooking. It just happened that one night my parents ordered pizza from the same place I was at when I heard about Michael. As soon as I took a bite of my slice, I was pulled back. But not to a single moment like for you and your halmunee, and like how I can do now. I had no idea what was happening. No one ever taught me how to do it and control it. So I was pulled from one moment to the next. The best and worst times I'd ever shared with Michael. It was crazy, and really scary. I couldn't stop it."

Jeff paused, and Maya stared at his profile. She couldn't even imagine how hard that must have been. Her first trip back was relatively easy compared to what he must have experienced, and that had been enough to terrify her. She also had Halmunee with her on all those trips. Jeff was alone.

"I was tearing through different dimensions and I thought I was going crazy. Then, something good finally happened. I was about to give up when I landed here and everything just stopped. I was lucky that another traveler had seen me. He said I was blinking on and off by my tree. He grabbed me and held me in place. It was the first moment of calm in what felt like forever. It was safe here. And after a while I was able to figure out how to control it and went back to my time. It still happened and tripped me up sometimes, but it slowly got better and easier. And soon I was able to find others on my own."

"How?" asked Maya.

Jeff gestured above them. "Through the trees. A couple times I've run into different travelers in the orchard. They come from all different times! But it was the first traveler that had stopped me that told me about traveling through other trees. He didn't have the same abilities as us, but he was very familiar with the orchard as he had been searching for someone for a long time. I can't do it with everyone though. I'm still practicing. I usually have to have a connection with someone and know where their tree is."

"How did you find my tree? Or was it my halmunee's tree?"

"You forget that the first time you met me wasn't the first time I had met you," said Jeff. "And I can ask the tree for a persimmon, but there's no guarantee that it will respond or give me the right moment. I've gotten better over time. And it helps when there's something specific I can ask for."

"Like my red red sweater?" Maya asked.

Jeff smiled for the first time in a long time, and it immediately put Maya more at ease.

"Yes," he said. "Like your red red sweater."

"So maybe next time I'll wear a blue blue sweater?"

This made Jeff laugh, and Maya felt a small bit of pleasure at having made him feel better. As much as his silliness annoyed her at times, it was infinitely preferable to Jeff being angry and sad.

"Or maybe you can wear a crazy crazy hat," said Jeff.

"My friend has one with animal ears. Or maybe one with pompoms?"

"I was thinking more of an umbrella hat."

"You know," said Maya, "I totally would have one of those, but it never rains enough in California."

At this point, they were both snorting with laughter.

"Come on," said Jeff, standing and helping Maya up. "We should get back to your halmunee. It's not good to spend so much time here. I don't think any person is meant to spend too long here."

Maya nodded and wrapped her arms around herself. The place was beautiful, but a little spooky. The eerie silence and darkness reminded her that there was nothing living here. Well, nothing other than the trees. And she wasn't sure if they were really alive. Past, present, and future remained frozen in the trees.

"Jeff?"

"Yeah?"

"If the birthday party wasn't the first time you met me, that means that I haven't gotten to that moment yet. I mean, the first time you met me hasn't happened for me yet. So, when will it happen?"

Jeff nudged her with his elbow. "I can't tell you. Where's the fun in that?"

"Oh, come on."

"Nope." Jeff continued before Maya could protest again. "Some things you're meant to know at certain times. Hey, next time let's meet back at the picnic if you can. I like that spot."

Maya gave up pestering Jeff for more information and smiled at him.

"I'll wear something blue blue."

CHAPTER 16

INSIDE JOKE

Every day after school, Maya rushed home to bake in the hope that she'd manage to time-travel by herself. Instead of trying a variety of foods and memories, she decided to focus on one specific one. She picked one that she could replicate with minimal work and time: SDC cookies.

After making large batches of cookie dough, she divided them up into individual tablespoon-sized balls, flash-froze them, and then stored them in the freezer. Freezing the dough meant that she could bake a batch of cookies anytime and they would still be perfectly warm and gooey-fresh from the oven. Whenever she had a free moment, she took a serving or two out, baked them, and tried to revisit the time she first had the famous SDC cookies at Jada's house.

But so far she hadn't had any success on her own.

"Is there a bake sale going on at school?"

Mom had wandered into the kitchen and was eyeing the mess on the kitchen counter.

"Huh?" Maya concentrated on scooping and leveling several cups of flour into a large bowl. "What? Oh, no. I just felt like making something. You know, like how we used to."

"Hmm," Mom said as she poured herself a glass of wine.

Maya lost count of how many cups of flour she'd poured into the bowl. Sighing, she dropped the measuring cup on the counter and poured the flour back into the bag to start over. Something made her stop and look at Mom.

A faint memory scratched at the back of Maya's mind. A time from when she was so little she could sit on the kitchen counter and swing her legs against the tops of the wooden cupboard doors as she watched Mom cook. She recalled the feeling of pride as she helped by handing Mom whatever ingredients were within reach.

"Mom..."

Mom turned back to Maya before heading out of the kitchen. "Yes?"

Gathering up the courage to ask a question, Maya scratched nervously at her cheek, and a puff of flour settled over her face. "Do you want to maybe make something together?"

"Oh, Maya," said Mom, "I'm too tired to stand around in the kitchen all night. Maybe another day."

"Okay." Maya tried to keep the disappointment out of her voice. She'd felt so disconnected from Mom recently. It hadn't bothered her so much at first. She'd gotten used to it and settled into her usual routine. She knew Mom loved her, but that didn't necessarily mean they expressed it to each other or hung out together. But now that she was spending so much time with Halmunee and learning more about her, Maya felt the gap between her and Mom widening each day.

Did Mom even really know her anymore? Did she even know Mom? Had she ever known Mom?

"I just thought it might be nice," Maya said. "Like when I was little. How come we don't do that anymore? How come you don't cook as much as you used to?" Maya thought of the numerous missing pieces to the Dad puzzle. "Maybe you could show me how to make Dad's favorite food? I don't think I even know what his favorite food was. What was it?"

"I told you, he loved everything."

"But what was his absolute favorite? Or favorite snack?"

Mom looked out the window. She was quiet and still for so long, Maya didn't know if she should say something to catch Mom's attention again. But finally, after a long sigh, Mom spoke.

"It's hard to imagine it here in California, but your father loved when it got cold and snowed. His favorite snack was hotteok."

"Hotteok?" Maya had never heard of this food before.

"They're like pancakes with a sweet filling," said Mom.

"Like donuts?"

Mom laughed. "Kind of. But better. Street vendors would sell them hot and freshly made. Your father couldn't walk by one without getting one for himself and one for you."

"Those sound yummy," said Maya. "Could we make them ourselves? Could you show me?"

Mom turned to look at Maya. She seemed far away and lost in thought. With a slight shake of her head, she returned to her normal mode.

"I don't think so. I had a long day at work. I don't have the time or energy to bake right now."

Mom had always worked a full-time job at a small law firm, even when Maya was little, but she still used to cook every now and then, at least until the day Halmunee arrived and Mom started working longer hours. But Maya knew better than to make that point with Mom right now.

"I was just wondering," said Maya. "But never mind."

Mom gave Maya a small smile. "Like I said, maybe another day."

But Maya knew that day would never come. It was just a way to say no without really saying no.

She watched Mom leave the kitchen and regretted how she'd approached the situation.

She wished so badly that she could talk to Jada about this and tell her all about Halmunee and Jeff. But she couldn't. Not yet.

Once Maya mastered the art of time-traveling herself, she could bring Jada back and show her the truth and get some advice.

And then she could show Mom.

And now, she had a potential food memory of her own to unlock. Maya had a faint recollection of eating something sweet while sitting up high somewhere, maybe on Dad's shoulders. It must have been hotteok. Now she just needed a recipe.

Maya skipped out of the kitchen and to Halmunee's room.

"Where are you going in such a rush?" asked Halmunee as Maya slid through the door.

"How do you make hotteok?"

Halmunee frowned. "Hotteok? Now? No, it's too early."

Maya hadn't expected Halmunee to refuse.

"Why not now?"

"Because." Halmunee paused and looked around the room and

then out the window. "Because you have to wait for it to get cold and snow."

Maya's shoulders drooped. "But it doesn't snow here. And why does it matter?"

But Halmunee had her mind set and a stubborn expression on her face.

"No. It has to be cold and snow. We'll get some snow in the winter. It always snows here in Seoul. Now, go to school. You're running late."

Maya wanted to push further but Halmunee was getting confused and disoriented. It was after school, and they most definitely were not in Seoul. So Maya would have to find another way.

After a quick search online, Maya found a couple recipes for hotteok and chose the one with photos, figuring it would be easier to follow.

The next day after school, Maya immediately set out to try making hotteok while Halmunee was napping and before Mom came home from work. But her hotteok didn't come out right. Not the first time, not the second time, and not even the third time. First she burned it, then she undercooked it, and then she put too much filling inside. Before she could try a fourth time, Halmunee woke from her nap and she had to hurry up and clean. She would keep trying.

But school and friends got in the way. Jada had been getting increasingly annoyed the past few weeks at how busy and distant Maya was.

"You've skipped the past two project meetings," said Jada. Maya knew this was serious because Jada had actually called her instead of just texting like usual. "Have you even started any of the drawings? Izzy needs to know the size and number for the layout."

"I know," said Maya. "Izzy has been texting me practically every day. You know how crazy she can get."

"Actually, I'm on Izzy's side on this," said Jada. "My, you're my friend and I love you, but you can't keep bailing like this. This is fifty percent of my grade too, you know."

"I'm sorry," said Maya. "I've just been so busy with family stuff."

"I get it," said Jada. "But you can't be busy all the time. What about today? We're going shopping for supplies and then hanging out at Emma's house afterward. My mom can pick you up along the way."

Maya knew she hadn't been a very good friend or classmate lately, but she kept telling herself that once she figured out how to travel back by herself, she could explain what was going on to Jada and fix everything. There'd be no more reason to keep secrets and she could focus more on schoolwork and her friends. It had been so long since she had been Friend Maya to Jada, she hoped she hadn't lost her completely.

"Okay," said Maya.

An hour later, Maya was sitting outside waiting for Jada. When a familiar green minivan pulled up to the curb, Maya hopped in and greeted Jada's mom. A few minutes later, Mrs. Williams dropped them off at the shopping mall and was waved goodbye.

"Can we do a quick stop at Kitschy Kitchen before we meet up with Emma and Izzy?" asked Maya. "I need to get an apron."

Maya's laundry pile was getting bigger and bigger as she kept messing up her clothes while baking. There was enough flour on all her shirts to probably fill up a bag.

"An apron?" asked Jada.

"Yeah. I've been doing a lot of cooking recently."

Jada shrugged. "Sure. We're a little early anyways."

They walked in silence toward the store.

Normally they'd be chatting or joking, but there was a slight tension in the air between them. It had been a while since they'd hung out outside of school, and even longer since they'd gone shopping together.

By the time they left the Kitschy Kitchen with bags in hand, things had lightened up and they were trading the latest gossip. Maya was so engrossed in Jada's story about her recent project date with Emma, she almost missed it.

"Oh," she said, grabbing Jada's arm. "Can we stop in here for a second?"

Jada looked at the store window and then at Maya. "Caps? You want to go in there? I didn't think you were a big hat wearer."

"I'm not," said Maya. "It's just that I have to get that umbrella hat."

"For real?"

"Just for fun. It's a joke I have with—um, with someone."

"Oh, yeah?" Jada frowned. "An inside joke? With who?"

"Um, my grandmother," Maya said nervously. The lie slipped out before she could stop it. She was amazed at how easy it was to deceive her best friend. "She's been feeling down lately. I can just run in and get it real quickly if you don't want to go inside. I'll be back."

Before Jada could ask any more questions, Maya ran into the store and picked up an umbrella hat on her way to the register. At least they'd be meeting Izzy and Emma soon so she'd only have to stall Jada's questions for a little bit.

She wished she hadn't said anything. She hated keeping secrets from Jada.

But, staring at the ridiculous hat, Maya couldn't wait to see Jeff's reaction. She just knew it would crack him up.

If she ever managed to make a trip back again.

CHAPTER 17

TOSSING COOKIES

A week later, Jada came over to Maya's house to hang out while their parents had dinner together and Jada's brothers were sleeping over at a friend's house. Maya and Jada had been such close friends for so long, it was inevitable that a friendship would also bloom between Maya's mother and Jada's parents. They were probably the only friends Mom really had, or at least the only ones Maya knew about. They made an effort to go out together every other week.

Jada had acted a little odd toward the end of their trip to the mall, but she seemed okay by the time they got to Emma's house. That might have been because she was distracted by Emma, though. Maya wanted to make sure things were still good between Jada and her. She made sure the refrigerator was stocked with Jada's favorite cherry soda and bought a small set of colorful nail polishes and stickers that she knew Jada would love. They could have a relaxing, fun night of watching a movie and doing their nails. Maya was determined not to lose her best friend.

Halmunee was still not feeling well and had gone to bed early with a lingering cough. Maya was a little relieved, as evenings were usually more challenging for Halmunee. She often got increasingly confused or agitated as the night went on.

"Don't you have anything good to eat in here?" Jada shut the pantry door, rejoined Maya in the living room, and plopped onto the sofa.

"You know how my mom and grandmother are," said Maya.

"We're growing girls! We need the essential food groups: chocolate, cookies, chips, and candy." Jada picked up one of the many pillows Mom couldn't stop buying that were taking up all the space on the sofa and chairs.

"Oh, I just remembered." Maya moved Gizmo off her lap and jumped off the sofa. "I do have something good to eat," she yelled over her shoulder.

"Oh, yeah?" Jada asked, trailing after Maya. "What?"

"Cookies!"

"What kind of cookies are we talking about here?" asked Jada. "SDC?"

"Of course SDC," said Maya. "As if there's any better cookie out there. There's just one slight issue."

Jada raised an eyebrow. "What?"

"We need to make them!" Maya held up a bag of flour and a bag of chocolate chips.

Jada groaned but she joined Maya in the kitchen.

"I'm only doing this if I get to eat the leftover cookie dough from the bowl afterwards," said Jada. "Ugh, we're not going to have time to refrigerate the dough too. You know that makes a big difference!"

Maya let Jada continue to grumble as she got out the mixer.

By the time she had finished mixing the butter and sugar together into a crystallized, sticky dough, Jada was happily munching on the chocolate chips as she cut a piece of parchment paper for the baking sheet. Whenever they made SDC cookies at Maya's house, Jada let Maya take the lead, even though she sometimes couldn't resist telling Maya what to do.

"Fold the flour in gently," said Jada.

"I know," said Maya.

"I'm just making sure you're honoring the SDC recipe," said Jada.

Maya picked up a chocolate chip and threw it at Jada, who deftly caught it in her mouth.

"You can't out-cookie me!" Jada laughed.

Maya was tempted to throw a handful of chocolate chips at Jada, but she didn't want to risk Gizmo rushing in to gobble them up.

Instead, she placed the parchment paper on the baking sheet and scooped up small balls of cookie dough.

As the cookies baked, the kitchen filled with the sugary-sweet aroma of chocolate melting into the buttery dough. The tiniest hint of vanilla extract in the cookie dough carried a surprisingly strong scent as the bottoms of the cookies browned and crisped.

"I'll never forget the first time your dad baked these cookies for us," Maya said, smiling at Jada. "They tasted like little pieces of heaven. I'd never had anything as good before."

Jada laughed as Maya pulled the cookies out of the oven and set them on a rack to cool. "I remember. You actually closed your eyes as you ate that first cookie. And then the second cookie. And then the third cookie."

"Okay, okay," Maya said, laughing with Jada. "What can I say? I love cookies, and the SDC cookies were the best ones I'd ever tasted."

"Can't argue with that," said Jada. She leaned over the cookies and inhaled deeply. "Think they're cool enough now? Do we risk burning our fingers and tongues, or do we wait a few more minutes? What do you think?"

Jada and Maya looked at each other and at the same time yelled, "Risk it!"

They eagerly picked out the biggest cookies, handling them gingerly with their fingertips. Out of habit, Maya closed her eyes just as she bit into the warm, soft cookie. Despite the numerous cookies Maya had been eating the past few weeks, she still enjoyed every single one. There was nothing quite like a freshly baked cookie, just cool enough to be picked off the rack. And eating the cookies with Jada made it more fun. They tasted even more delicious than when eating them alone, frustrated by her inability to travel back in time on her own.

"SDC cookies kick butt!" said Jada as she devoured her first one. She picked up a second one and passed it back and forth between her hands. "Look, Maya. I'm tossing my cookies!"

Maya groaned. "Tossing cookies? That hasn't been funny since the first time you made that joke."

Maya gave Jada a playful poke. As soon as her fingers touched Jada's arm, something pulled at her from behind, making her stumble.

"What was that?" asked Jada, frowning.

Maya stared up at her, unable to say a word, and then looked back at the cookie in her hand. Taking another bite and savoring the smooth chocolate on her tongue, Maya reached out and gripped Jada's arm tightly. She closed her eyes and thought back to the first time Jada had made that stupid joke, while they had been eating the cookies that Mr. Williams had pulled out fresh from the oven.

Maya concentrated on the fine details of that moment. She pictured in her head the blue shirt and shorts she had been wearing, and Jada's red-and-black outfit that had matched the ties in her hair. Mr. Williams had been wearing a crisp white shirt with not a single spot or stain anywhere. He had slapped their hands away from the hot cookie sheet, warning the girls to keep away or he'd make them wait in Jada's room until everything was ready. Maya had peered down and analyzed the large crystals of salt sitting on top of the cookies, and had asked why the sugar hadn't melted.

A shaky hand grabbed Maya's other arm.

"My? My? What's going on?" A tremor ran through Jada's voice, dragging out the vowels of her words.

Maya opened her eyes.

She'd done it.

She was there.

She was here.

SDC COOKIES

By Jada

~~~~~~~~~~

¾ cup granulated sugar

¾ cup packed brown sugar

½ cup salted butter, softened to room temperature

2 large eggs, room temperature

1 teaspoon vanilla extract

1 teaspoon sea salt, plus more for sprinkling

1 teaspoon baking soda

2 ¼ cups all-purpose flour

2 cups bittersweet chocolate chips

1. Mix the granulated and brown sugars in a large bowl.

2. Mix the butter into the sugars.

3. Add the eggs and stir the mixture together.

4. Add the vanilla extract, salt, and baking soda. Mix well.

5. Add the flour and mix just enough to incorporate the flour into the dough.

6. Fold the chocolate chips into the dough.

7. Wrap the dough tightly and refrigerate for 24–36 hours. You don't have to do this, but it makes the cookies taste way better!

8. When ready to bake, preheat oven to 375 degrees Fahrenheit and line a cookie sheet with parchment paper.

9. Scoop small balls of dough onto your lined cookie sheet, about 2 inches apart. Sprinkle a tiny bit of sea salt on top of the cookie balls.

10. Bake for 9–11 minutes, until the edges start to look golden brown.

11. Take cookies out of oven and let them cool for a few minutes on the cookie sheet and then on a cooling rack.

12. Keep baking more batches!

CHAPTER 18

NO MORE SECRETS

Maya and Jada stood in the middle of Jada's old kitchen, before it was renovated a few years ago. Younger versions of Jada and Maya were in front of them, giggling as they made silly faces at each other. They had pushed their chairs away from the table so that they leaned against the counter, where a cooling rack had been set out. Kneeling on the seats of their chairs, they waited as Mr. Williams slipped on a pair of oven mitts.

"Keep back until I say they're ready," said Mr. Williams as he bent over and opened the oven door. A wave of heat hit the girls' faces, making them shut their eyes. Carefully, he set the cookie sheet on top of the cooling rack. At the sound of the cookie sheet hitting the metal slats, the girls' eyes opened wide and their hands darted out.

"I said keep back. They're too hot." Mr. Williams slapped the girls' outstretched hands away. "When I say they're ready, you can each take one."

"Thank you, Mr. Williams," said little Maya. Parents always loved Maya because she was so polite. And Maya loved Mr. Williams as the father she didn't have. "These smell so good!"

"Daddy makes the best cookies in the whole wide world!" Little Jada puffed up with pride and tried to sneak a cookie, but Mr. Williams had eyes in the back of his head and turned around to slap her hand away again.

"What did I say?!"

"It's so hard waiting!" Jada pouted.

"If you try that one more time, I'm sending both of you to your room to wait until the cookies are properly cooled."

Maya peered closely at the cookies, keeping her hands behind her back. "Why is there still sugar on top?"

"That's not sugar," said Mr. Williams. "That's salt. It brings out the best in these cookies. You'll see."

Standing just to the side of the counter, Maya looked back and forth between the younger versions of herself and Jada.

I've done it, she thought to herself. *I've finally done it.*

After a small kitchen timer went off, Mr. Williams gave the girls permission to pick up their cookies. Just as Jada had remembered, little Maya closed her eyes as she bit into the large, warm cookie.

A sharp pain pulled Maya out of her daze. Jada's grip on her arm tightened.

"My, what is this?" she whispered. "Is this some sort of prank? How is this possible?"

A wave of guilt washed over Maya. She'd been so ecstatic that she'd finally succeeded, she hadn't thought about how Jada must be feeling. And it hadn't been so long ago that Maya had suffered the same shock of her own first trip back. She didn't have to try hard to imagine the panic and fear Jada must be feeling.

"Oh, Jay," said Maya, "I'm sorry, but everything is okay. Everything's great, in fact. I know this seems crazy, but it's all completely normal. I mean, relatively normal. Normal for this." She gestured to the younger versions of themselves and Mr. Williams.

Jada gulped a few times, her eyes darting nervously as she took in the entire scene. Maya's words appeared not to have comforted her at all.

"I can explain everything," Maya persisted. "But please try to keep calm. And—"

She was interrupted by a phone ringing close by. Mr. Williams wiped his hands on his pants and headed in their direction to answer it. As he brushed past them, he passed right through Jada's side. Jada's mouth formed a perfect circle and her hands flew up to her face in horror.

"No," Maya cried out. "Don't let go of me."

But it was too late. Jada was gone.

Great. Now what was Maya supposed to do? This was her first time traveling by herself, and she was anxious about returning to the present without Halmunee to guide her. Maya looked at the younger versions of herself and Jada, chocolate smeared all over their hands and faces as they continued to gorge on cookies while Mr. Williams was on the phone. He would be off the phone soon, and then he would return and shoo the girls away to clean themselves up.

Maya just hoped that Jada would still be there when she returned home. And she hoped that her friend would understand.

"Look, Maya! I'm tossing my cookies!" Jada joked as she threw several cookies in the air. Maya burst into giggles and reached for the fallen cookies to copy her friend.

"What are you doing?" cried Mr. Williams. He had returned to the kitchen and was staring aghast at the mess Maya and Jada had made, and the sheer volume of cookies they had managed to eat in a matter of minutes. "Don't touch anything! Both of you, come here and wash your hands and faces. Jada, don't you dare take another cookie. Put it down. Now!"

Jada hesitated, but then, huffing dramatically, she finally put down her cookie and trudged over to the sink. Maya followed her friend, practically vibrating from the unfamiliar rush of sugar coursing through her body.

Maya heard the faucet being turned on and then, without any warning, was pulled back to the present, standing in her kitchen and facing a stunned Jada.

"My!" Jada cringed. "You scared me! One second you're missing and the next you pop out of nowhere!"

Tentatively, Jada reached out and touched Maya's arm as if to make sure she was real. She breathed a sigh of relief when she felt her fingers make contact with Maya's skin instead of passing through her, like what had happened just a few minutes before.

"This is real?" asked Jada.

"Yes," said Maya. "And so was that." Then the words poured out of her in excitement and relief. "It's what I've been keeping secret from you. I've wanted to tell you, but I didn't think you'd believe me. I wanted to wait until I could show you."

The startled look on Jada's face faded into one of anger. "Thanks for the heads-up! You could have given me some warning before doing that . . . that . . . whatever it was that you did."

Jada turned to leave. Maya raced around the counter and held out her hands to stop her.

"I'm sorry," said Maya. "I'm really, really sorry. I didn't mean to. It just came on so suddenly while we were eating and laughing and talking about that first time I had these cookies." Maya gripped Jada's arms. "But don't you see? Now I can tell you. Now you'll understand. You know, that thing I just did? I took us back into the past."

"My," Jada said slowly, doubt creeping into her voice. "Time travel doesn't exist. It's not possible in real life."

Exasperated, Maya threw her hands up in the air. "What do you think we just did? How else do you explain it? And I'm not the only one who can do it. Well, I mean I wasn't even able to do it on my own until just now. But Jeff told me if I practiced enough, I'd get there—that I have the natural power and skill. Oh, and now I can tell you all about Jeff!"

Jada held up her hands and shook her head. "Whoa, whoa, whoa. Slow down. You're unleashing a whole lot of crazy on me all at once."

Maya's excitement faded. "I'm not crazy," she whispered. "You saw."

Jada gently steered Maya to a chair. "That's not what I meant. Let's sit down and then you can tell me everything. And I mean everything. No more secrets anymore. And promise you won't do anything like that again without warning me first. I don't think I can handle two trips like that in one night."

And so Maya sat down and, as they ate the rest of the cookies they'd baked, she told her best friend everything.

CHAPTER 19

TWO LISTS

Jada didn't say a word as Maya told her all about the first few trips with Halmunee. Maya was so relieved to be able to finally talk about what had been happening these past months. The words tumbled out of her as she described all the things she'd seen, and her later trips when she met with Jeff.

Only when she finished did Jada speak. "Well, I understand now why you didn't want to tell me anything at first. I don't know if I would have believed it if I hadn't seen it myself." Jada shivered. "It's spooky. When my dad passed right through me, I thought for a second that I had died or something and turned into a ghost."

"I'm sorry," said Maya. "I didn't mean to scare you like that."

"I'll recover." Jada fell back in her chair, the back of her hand pressed against her forehead in a dramatic pose.

Maya smiled. If Jada was joking around again that meant she wasn't mad or freaked out by her.

Quickly shifting positions, Jada sat up and shook a finger at Maya. "But seriously, don't ever do that again without giving me warning!"

"I promise, I won't!"

"And I don't know if I want to do that again anyways." Jada paused for a few seconds before continuing. "Well, maybe not for a while. Let me think about it. It might be fun to go back and do things a little differently."

"No," said Maya. "It doesn't work like that. We can't change the past or talk with anyone there. It's like how it was back in your house. Nobody could see, hear, or touch us, remember?"

Jada frowned. "So, you can go back, but you can't really do anything. Well then, what's the point? Why keep going back?"

Maya paused. How could she explain this to Jada in a way that would make her understand?

Sometimes, just seeing someone or being someplace was enough. Maya knew that was how Halmunee felt about Harabujee, her mother, and everything and everyone else in her past.

Maya would give anything to spend time following after Dad, studying everything about him, from his annoying habits to the things that made him laugh. And with enough practice, maybe one day Maya would be able to find him. If not from the fleeting moments in her own past when their paths intersected, then in the orchard.

"Well," Maya started hesitantly, "the first couple times, I didn't really have much of a say. I got pulled in like you just did. And then I wanted to keep going back to find out what this was. You have the benefit of having me to tell you all about it. My grandmother tells me things in bits and pieces when she can, but it's never a full picture and it's always confusing. She seems to get comfort from it, especially since her memory is starting to go. I think it helps her to actually watch the scenes from her past. And I can't stop feeling like she's trying to show me something. Something important."

"And you also met Jeff," said Jada.

"Yes, and then I met Jeff. But it's not like that. It's because of what he told me. That maybe over time I can learn how to cross the different dimensions, meet more people that are like us, be able to step into any moment in the past, not just a memory of mine or my grandmother's. I mean, how amazing would that be?"

"But you can't do anything when you're there," Jada said. "You told me you can't change the past."

"I know," said Maya. "Yes, there are things I'd love to change, but then nothing would be the same. I wouldn't be the same. But I could go back and get to know some people from my past. Like my dad."

Jada stopped in the middle of biting down on her last cookie. She wiped the crumbs off her mouth and swallowed. "Oh, My. I hadn't thought of that. Of course."

Maya looked away and shrugged. "Well, it's not like I can even do any of that at this point. First, I need to learn how to go back whenever I want and be able to find Jeff so that he can teach me how to do what he does."

Tapping a finger on her chin, Jada frowned as she looked off into the distance. "So how do you know how to find him? And how did he find you?"

"He won't tell me!" Maya groaned and slumped back in her chair. "He said the first time I met him wasn't the first time he met me. So that means it hasn't happened yet, and he won't tell me about it because he says it will ruin the surprise."

"What?"

"I know!" Maya dropped her head into her hands. "He can be very frustrating."

Jada poked Maya's head until she looked up. She had the crazy glint in her eye that meant her brain was working overtime. She might not always have had the grades to prove it, but she was so smart that Maya struggled to keep up with her sometimes. Granted, it was often because she was going down random trains of thought and expecting everyone else to be able to follow her seemingly unconnected jumps in logic. But that was also what made her kind of brilliant. She was able to see the connections between things that no one else did.

"Well, let's make everything clear. We'll make two lists." She pulled out a notepad and pen from her bag and drew a line down the middle of the page.

"So, from what you've told me, you have two problems—what your grandmother is trying to show you and how to find Jeff."

Jada wrote GRANDMOTHER at the top of the left column and JEFF at the top of the right column.

"With your grandmother, let's make a list of all the times you've visited the past with her."

Maya recounted all her trips back, and Jada made brief notes for each trip.

Staring at the list, Jada chewed on her pen, adding a fresh layer of teeth marks to the already mangled end. "Well, I can't see any trend here. Of course, the picnic was one you suggested. And it sounds like she took you back to the birthday celebration just because she felt like revisiting a happy moment from her past with her friends and family." Jada tossed the notepad across the counter to Maya. "Take a look for yourself. Maybe there's nothing here. Maybe your grandmother is just feeling nostalgic for the old times and wants to revisit her favorite memories. Maybe this is just all part of her teaching you how to travel back like she does."

Maya shook her head and, after a quick glance, slid the notebook back to Jada. "No. I don't think that's it. I mean, I don't think that's the only reason."

"What about your mom?" asked Jada. "Have you tried asking her? You can take her with you now and show her. She'll have to believe you now."

Maya hesitated before answering. That had been the original plan. And yet, she was nervous at the thought of bringing this to Mom now.

Mom and Halmunee had a fairly strained relationship. What with the added stress of Halmunee's illness, Maya didn't want to cause more trouble if it could be avoided. And her relationship with Mom had chilled this past year. Mom was either too exhausted or too distracted to pay any attention to Maya. And would Mom understand about her need to find Dad? Would Mom dissuade her or try to prevent her from finding his tree? Would she tell her not to dwell on the past and to focus on her life here and now?

"No," said Maya. "My grandmother said this ability skips around in families. And I'm not ready yet to show her. I want to find out more about what this is before I bring her in."

"Then you need to get more info," said Jada. "You need to take more trips with your grandmother and get her to talk more."

"All right," said Maya. "That sounds like a good game plan.

Grandmother. More visits. More talking."

"Now, on to Jeff." Jada looked down at her list. "Okay, Jeff is obviously short for Jeffrey, right? Is it J-E-F-F, or G-E-O-F-F? Or something else? Do you know his last name?"

Maya shook her head.

"Do you know where he lives?"

Maya shook her head again.

"Do you have his phone number? His email address? Social media? Anything?"

"Sorry." Maya shrugged.

Jada shook her pen at Maya. "I need something that will help our search. Names. Places. Events."

Maya thought back to all her visits with Jeff and sifted through the details for any tidbits of information about him.

"Oh," she said. "He said he lives in the DC area. And he runs. He mentioned something about running a half-marathon. And he has at least two brothers, one older and one younger. His younger brother, Michael, died in a car accident when he was nine. I don't know about the rest of his family though. I think they're Korean, or at least he speaks Korean with a better accent than I do."

After Jada wrote down these facts, she pressed for additional details. "Maya, I really need something more to get started. At least a last name. 'Jeff' is too common of a first name. You get me his last name and I'll find him for you."

Suddenly Jada dropped her pen and stared at Maya, her mouth hanging open. "It's Jeff, isn't it?"

Maya tilted her head quizzically. "Um, yeah. His name is Jeff. We were just talking about that."

"No," said Jada. "I mean, it was Jeff you bought that umbrella hat for, right?"

Maya laughed. "Yeah. But I haven't shown him yet."

Jada hooted in laughter. "This is perfect. You're both such dorks!"

Also laughing, Maya grabbed the pen and threw it at Jada.

"It's not like that," said Maya. "We're just good friends."

"So he's no David, then," said Jada as she threw the pen back at Maya.

This went on for a few more rounds.

"But seriously," said Jada. "I'm glad you told me everything. I knew something wasn't right."

"You don't know how good it feels to finally tell you."

Maya felt Friend Maya settling comfortably next to Family Maya, both making room for each other, as she and Jada talked and laughed together for the rest of the night.

CHAPTER 20

BLUE BLUE

A couple days later, Mom worked late and Halmunee, still not feeling well, went to bed early again. After heating up some frozen food for dinner, Maya settled at the kitchen table to finish her homework, with Gizmo snoring at her feet. She was halfway through her math assignment when her brain started going fuzzy and she knew she needed a break. She took out her phone and texted Jada.

It didn't take long before Jada responded.

JADA: what's up?

MAYA: slowly dying under a pile of homework

JADA: BORING
       update on jeff?

MAYA: no

JADA: any more trips back?

MAYA: no...

JADA: why not?? gogogo!

Now that Jada had gotten it into Maya's head, she couldn't concentrate on her homework at all. All she could think about was traveling back.

After all, she could do it now; she could go back on her own.

Why hadn't she tried it over the weekend? She had made some more gimbap just yesterday to try to go back to the picnic. Jeff had said she could find him anytime she needed him.

What was she waiting for?

Maya closed her books and went to her room to fetch her favorite blue sweater and the crazy rainbow-colored umbrella hat she'd bought with Jada. She crammed them into the bag with her sketchbook and art supplies. An eager Gizmo trailing after her in anticipation, she returned to the kitchen and headed to the refrigerator. She took out the container of gimbap and tossed some of the beef and egg from one of the pieces into his bowl.

As her teeth sank into the cold gimbap, she thought back to the day when a young Halmunee gathered with her schoolmates for a picnic. It was funny how an event that happened before Maya was even born was now a memory of her very own.

Nothing happened at first. She closed her eyes to focus and visualize the scene. The brilliant blue of the sky without a single cloud to dampen the brightness of the sun; the smooth, round green hills of the ancient tombs; the small T-shaped shrine that sat at the base of the tomb where she was going to look for Jeff.

It was a bit slower this time, but eventually Maya was pulled back into the familiar warmth of the strong sun on her face and arms, and the loud laughter and chatter of girls excited to have a day away from school.

She opened her eyes and watched as the girls split into smaller groups of friends and opened up their packs filled with gimbap and hard-boiled eggs. It felt good to be outside on a beautiful sunny day that felt like summer break.

She peered at Hyun Suk's group and then at the cluster of trees nearby, looking for any sign of the past visit she and Halmunee had made. She knew that they were in separate dimensions, but she wondered if she might see something, a shimmer or shadow, that would hint at the other versions of herself and Halmunee. But there wasn't a thing to see.

She made her way slowly up one of the hills, looking for Jeff.

When Maya reached the top, she found that she was alone. Even though Maya knew no one could see her, she felt a bit ridiculous putting on the umbrella hat. She wandered around the top of the hill, calling out Jeff's name.

Suddenly, she heard someone snorting behind her.

Maya turned just as Jeff cried out, "The hat! I can't believe you got the umbrella hat!" He burst into laughter.

"I thought that would catch your attention," said Maya, laughing with him.

"I was looking for a blue blue Maya, but this is even better."

"I probably should have saved it for our next meeting, but I couldn't resist." Maya pulled off the hat and smoothed her hair back into place. "Here, you take it. Maybe one day when I can do what you do, I'll find you for the first time with this hat."

"Well, maybe not the first time," said Jeff as he put on the hat, making both of them laugh again. "Maybe the second."

"I'll be expecting it now," said Maya.

"So, what were you doing anyways when you called me?" Jeff asked. He took off the hat and folded it under his arm.

"I was wondering if I could see some sort of a hint of me and my halmunee from our last visit."

"And did you?"

Maya sighed. "No. Nothing." She turned to Jeff and grinned. "But I finally did it."

Jeff looked blankly at Maya. "Huh?"

Maya gestured to the picnicking groups. "No Halmunee. I made it here all by myself."

"What?" Jeff broke into a wide grin. "Already? You did it all on your own?"

His enthusiasm was so contagious, Maya got a boost of energy from it. "Yeah, and this isn't even my first time back. I had no idea how much energy and focus it takes, though."

"You'll get used to it," said Jeff. "You'll be better than me soon."

Maya shook her head. "I don't know if I'll ever be as good as you."

"Trust me. You'll definitely be better than me."

"I don't know if I'll be able to cross dimensions like you can," said Maya. "It was hard enough getting here on my own."

"What if I show you what it's like? Would you want to see?"

The idea of it frightened and excited her. Maya hesitated for a second before she said, "Yes."

Jeff held out his hand. "You know the way. At least this part."

Maya took his hand and prepared herself as Jeff pulled them into the abyss.

CHAPTER 21

JEFF'S PERSIMMON

Maya was relieved when her feet made contact with solid ground again and she could make out the distant lights of the orchard.

After knocking on the gate and waiting for it to swing open, Jeff and Maya entered the golden orchard. Still holding hands, Jeff pulled Maya along as they ran through the trees.

"Where are we going?" she called out.

"I'll know it when I find it," said Jeff.

They weaved between the trees until Maya grew dizzy and disoriented. They all looked the same to her. She didn't know how Jeff could tell the difference between any of them, but suddenly he slowed and rested his hand against the trunk of one of the trees.

"This is it," he said, gazing up at the jeweled orbs dangling high above in the branches.

"Whose tree is this?"

Jeff's gaze traveled down the tree and to Maya.

"It's, uh, it's my tree."

"Really?" Maya reached out to touch the glowing bark. She didn't know what she was expecting, but she was a little disappointed that she didn't feel anything different as she had with her own tree. "How did you find it just now?"

Jeff shrugged. "I just did. I can't explain it. It's like that feeling you get when you're on your way home after a long vacation. You know, as the car starts making familiar turns, even if you're half asleep or not paying attention at first, you just know."

"Yeah, like puppy-dog instincts. They always find their way back home."

"Yeah, just like that," Jeff said, nodding enthusiastically. "The more times I visit a tree, the easier it is to find it."

"So that's why we're using your tree? Because it's the easiest for you to find?"

"Well, that," admitted Jeff. "But also, I think it'll be easier to bring you along to one of my past moments, since we already know each other. It helps when you already have a connection."

"How do you find the others? Other people like us?"

"Well, our trees are a little different. A little unique. You see how mine twists and then splits?"

Jeff pointed up at the point of the trunk where it broke off into numerous branches. The trunk of the tree twisted as though it had been frozen mid-dance as it twirled in circles.

"Our trees aren't straight up and down like others," Jeff continued. "Because our lives aren't like that. Everyone else lives past, present, and then future. But we don't. Not really. For us, everything is more mixed together. Like our trees."

Maya studied Jeff's tree. The smooth bumps and ridges of the twists of Jeff's tree were like the tight tendons of a dancer's legs, capable of equal amounts of strength and flexibility. Her hand still on the trunk, she gazed at the other trees in the vicinity. Most were smooth and straight, but there were several clustered nearby that had similarly twisty trunks.

A rustle of leaves made Maya jump. She peered into the shadows. But the sound wasn't coming from a distance, it was coming from above. A thick, knobby branch lowered toward Jeff, as if the tree was bowing and asking him to dance. Several brilliant jeweled persimmons dangled from the branch, swaying from the movement.

Maya started to peer into the persimmon closest to her, but then drew back.

No. That would be wrong. These were Jeff's personal moments. She couldn't spy on them. She should wait for his invitation.

Jeff took a persimmon in his hand and turned to Maya. "This is the peach. I mean, persimmon to you. Are you ready?"

"Yes." Maya stepped to his side and held his hand.

"Don't let go," he said. "I don't know for sure if this will work. It might be as if you're a visitor, so you may need to keep holding onto me."

Maya braced herself. None of these trips had ever been easy, and she wasn't sure if this one would be like the others. But Maya didn't feel any of the violent jerks or jarring disorientation of the other trips. Instead, smoke curled around Jeff. He pulled her closer to him and the smoke tentatively reached out to her. It clouded her vision so she couldn't see, but the scent of freshly mowed grass filled the air. Maya took a deep breath and felt all the tension in her body melt away.

A loud crack rippled through the air, followed by the roar of a crowd.

"What was that?" she asked.

The smoke cleared enough for her to see Jeff by her side. He had a far-off look on his face that changed to a wide smile as he turned to Maya.

"It's baseball," he said. "Come on!"

They were running across a field of thick grass toward a baseball diamond. Everything looked weird, though. As if it was close and yet far away. Then Maya realized what it was.

"Little League!"

Two teams of little boys, probably first or second graders, were being cheered on by families and friends standing along the edges or sitting on blankets or folding chairs. The scoreboard showed that they were nearing the end of a tied game. The sun shone brightly in the clear blue sky. Maya tugged at the collar of her sweater, already starting to sweat from the heat. She held up her hand to shade her eyes.

"Want the umbrella hat?" Jeff asked.

Maya laughed. "No, it's yours now."

She scanned the teams for a younger version of Jeff. She thought she saw him. His ears seemed even bigger when he was younger.

"Is that you?" she asked, pointing at the little boy hovering on third base.

The expression on Jeff's face changed ever so slightly, with a tinge of sadness in his eyes. "No. That's not me."

"No way," protested Maya. "That's so you. Those are your ears!"

"Nope," said Jeff. "That's not me. That's Michael."

"Oh." Maya didn't know what else to say, so she said nothing more.

She studied Michael, his face screwed up in concentration as he squatted low, ready to run. Maya still couldn't believe that wasn't Jeff. They looked so alike. Her gaze drifted across the crowd as she searched for the Jeff from this moment. He had to be here. They were in his persimmon.

Another crack of a bat meeting a baseball, and Michael was off and running, his little arms pumping as hard as they could as he sped toward home plate. The moment he made it, he was immediately swept up by two older boys, Jeff and his other brother.

"Mikey, you did it!"

"You were great!"

Michael beamed up at his brothers. "We won! We won!"

"No duh," said the younger version of Jeff. He looked only a little younger than his current self, while his older brother looked to be in high school. "Dad will be so proud of you when he hears."

"Come on," said the older brother. He shook back his long, floppy hair from his face, the ends curling above the collar of his shirt. "I'll take you out for some ice cream."

"Shotgun!" Jeff and Michael cried out at the exact same time.

Jeff flicked the bill of Michael's hat. "Aw, man, you beat me again," he lied.

Michael beamed and skipped alongside his brothers. "Peach ice cream?"

"Of course," said Jeff. "Our favorite!"

"And can I get two scoops?" asked Michael.

"Sure," said the older brother. "And I'll even let you pick the music for our ride. Whatever tape you want."

Jeff's groan was cut short by a gruff voice calling out to them.

"Chung! Hey, Chung! Don't forget your mitt."

The coach tossed a baseball mitt to Michael.

"Good game."

"Thanks, Coach!" Michael waved goodbye and ran to catch up with his brothers.

As the three boys walked off, the purple haze returned, creeping across the grass until it swirled up and surrounded them. Maya tried waving the smoke away, but it grew so dense she could feel it resting against her skin, as if it were a dense fog.

When it finally thinned, she saw that they were back in the orchard, and the amethyst persimmon on the branch was already rising back to the treetop.

Still holding Jeff's hand, she turned to face him.

"So that was Michael?"

"Yeah. That was the last really good day we had with just the three of us. Me, Michael, and Patrick."

"That was a good day," Maya said. She would never know what it was like to have siblings, but everything about that moment had seemed perfect. "I'm glad you guys had it. And I'm glad you shared it with me."

"I wanted you to meet them," said Jeff. "And this is kind of like meeting them. In a way, you know."

The more Maya got to know Jeff, the more she wanted to know. Maya felt closer to him than she felt to most of her other friends (besides Jada, of course). She knew some of his deepest and most personal secrets, and yet she didn't know basic facts about him like exactly where he lived or what school he went to. Did he live in an apartment building or a house? Did he have a dog or cat or hamster?

Tentatively, Maya pressed forward, trying to push their friendship a little bit further. "I'd love to hear more about your family. We could exchange phone numbers or email addresses, or something like that."

"No," said Jeff. "Our phone connection isn't so great."

"Okay," said Maya. "What about email? It would be fun."

"Email? I don't know, Maya. I don't like mixing things up."

"Okay," Maya said slowly.

She didn't quite understand. Jeff had shown her his family, but he didn't want them to meet her? Maya felt like a part of Jada's family, a second daughter almost. She didn't have that many friends and it would be nice to have another one in her regular life.

"I guess I get it," Maya continued. "I mean, I have different worlds too: one where I'm Family Maya and the other where I'm Friend Maya. And it can be weird when those worlds interact. That's fine. But why can't we meet or talk outside of here?"

"Look, Maya," said Jeff, backing away, "I like hanging out with you here and all, but nothing more than that. Sorry."

Maya froze.

"We can meet and talk here because we've got the time for it," Jeff continued, avoiding making eye contact with her. "But I'm really busy back home. I need to focus on healing my knee so I can get back into training."

Maya frowned. Why was Jeff acting so weird and distant all of a sudden?

"I don't understand," said Maya. "Your knee? What does that have to do with anything?"

"It's nothing," Jeff said. "I just injured it a while ago when someone crashed into me, and I haven't been able to get back to race training just yet. And with school too . . . I'm just really busy. You're in California, and I'm in Virginia. We're on opposite coasts. It's best if we just keep things the way they are, okay?"

"Forget it then," said Maya. "I don't need you."

"Then stop pushing it, okay?"

Maya couldn't believe him. What was his problem? Was he trying to avoid her? But then why did he seek her out and why did he always seem eager to make plans for their next meeting?

Everything was going so wrong and Maya didn't know how to fix it. One minute she felt so close to Jeff, and the next she felt like she didn't even know him. She already put up with Mom pushing her away and keeping her distance. She didn't have to take it from him too.

Her face flushed as she balled up her fists. "Don't think you're so great and all. Forget I even asked. Just take me back to the picnic. I'll find my way home from there."

"Fine."

"Fine."

Jeff held out his hand and Maya reluctantly took it.

She wondered if this was the last time she'd ever see Jeff.

He's the one who doesn't want to be friends, she thought. *If he changes his mind, he can find me and apologize. I won't go looking for him. Ever.*

CHAPTER 22

SONGPYEON

A couple weeks later, the temperature dropped and fall announced its presence. Maya was still mad at Jeff and hadn't traveled back to the picnic since her last visit. Jada offered to find information about him, but Maya turned her down. If Jeff didn't want to be her friend, she didn't care a bit about him.

On a chilly day in November, Halmunee knocked on Maya's bedroom door and told her she wanted her help in making songpyeon.

When she saw Halmunee's eyes were clear and focused and her voice didn't quaver, Maya eagerly jumped out of bed and rushed to get ready. She wanted to take advantage of every good day Halmunee had left. She felt like she had wasted her past few trips with Jeff and had been neglecting her grandmother. She wouldn't make that mistake again. And she didn't need Jeff to help her find Dad. She'd do it on her own.

They put on some light coats and comfortable shoes and walked to the market. Maya loved trips to the Korean market. There were so many different foods and snacks, she felt she could spend hours wandering down the aisles and she'd still discover new things she'd never heard of before. Trips with Halmunee made Maya a little more anxious, though, because she always worried Halmunee might get confused and disoriented. But so far, they hadn't had a bad incident.

Halmunee also gave the best little tips as they passed by the produce.

"Best way to pick cantaloupe is to smell it and make sure the end is a little squishy when you push it."

"Garlic should always be firm. If it's too soft it's likely rotten inside."

"People always think the bigger the cucumber, the better. But no, that's wrong. Too big and it will be too bitter. Go for medium and bright green."

Maya nodded along as she pushed the shopping cart. She hoped to remember all this to write in her journal later, with colorful illustrations.

On their way back from the market, they made a short detour to a nearby park to collect some pine needles—an essential ingredient of the colorful stuffed rice cakes they planned to make.

"Why pine needles?" asked Maya.

She was trying to quickly grab handfuls without anyone else in the park noticing. But Halmunee shook them out of Maya's hand.

"No, these are no good. They're too old and dry. We need fresh pine needles. Climb onto that picnic table and see if you can reach that branch."

"But there are people here!" Maya was mortified at the thought.

"No one is watching you." Halmunee brushed away Maya's concerns. "The faster you do it the quicker it will be done."

Her cheeks red with embarrassment, Maya climbed onto the picnic table and jumped up to grab a handful of pine needles.

"More," said Halmunee.

Maya jumped again for more needles and then quickly climbed off the table.

"Hmm," said Halmunee. "I don't know if this will be enough."

"It's enough," said Maya as she rushed Halmunee out of the park.

Halmunee scoffed but allowed herself to be led away by Maya.

"Now we can make proper songpyeon," said Halmunee.

Song. Pyeon. Maya pictured the words trilled from a small and colorful bird on a bare branch. She had a love/hate relationship with songpyeon, the small and colorful rice cakes stuffed with different fillings. It all depended on which filling she got. Whenever Maya had eaten songpyeon in the past, she'd carefully select the ones she thought contained the sweet sesame filling. She tried poking at them, sniffing them, and looking closely at the seam where the dough was sealed up, but she could never accurately predict which ones had which fillings. There was no rhyme or reason. She could have three plump songpyeon, all the same color, each with a different filling. A tingle of satisfaction would run through her body as she bit the dough and the sweet sesame filling burst from within. But nothing was worse than sinking her teeth into the chewy dough only to continue through to a dense chestnut or red bean paste.

"We always make songpyeon for Chuseok," continued Halmunee, interrupting Maya's thoughts.

It was already November and they were long past the date of

Chuseok—the annual Korean harvest festival that happened in September or October, depending on the lunar calendar—but she didn't think such details were really necessary at this point. If Halmunee wanted to make songpyeon, they would make songpyeon. And Maya didn't want to break the news to Halmunee that Mom never made any; she just bought premade packs of them from the market whenever the craving hit. Those songpyeon were always slightly too chewy and greasy.

Truthfully, Maya and Mom didn't really celebrate Chuseok at all. Maya vaguely knew that it was essentially like a Korean version of Thanksgiving, when people spent time with their families, making and eating too much food. Though with Chuseok, there was the additional obligation of the visiting and clearing of ancestral graves.

When Maya was little and had asked Mom why they didn't celebrate Chuseok with their extended family, like Grace and Daniel Oh in her class, Mom had said that things were complicated with her family and she didn't like focusing on old traditions with bad memories. She said it in a way that almost made Maya feel guilty for even asking. She hadn't meant to bring up upsetting memories. But now Maya wanted more. She had never even met her grandmother until this past year. Who knew what other relatives she had?

After they got back home, they organized everything into three small stations. Each station had a large bowl with colored dough resting under plastic wrap—they'd used mugwort powder for the green, raspberry juice for the pink, and nothing for the white. With the dough ready to go, they turned their attention to the filling.

Halmunee ground roasted sesame seeds before mixing them with some honey and salt. Her hands were reassuringly strong and steady. "I don't know why you never liked those other fillings," she said to Maya, not missing a beat in her work. "They're good too."

Maya dipped her finger into the bowl and licked the sweet filling before Halmunee could slap her hand away. "No competition," she said. "This is the best one. Did Mom tell you this one was always my favorite?"

"Done!" Halmunee ignored Maya's question and gestured triumphantly at the bowl of completed filling. Maya shook her head and returned her focus to the work at hand.

Halmunee and Maya pulled apart the colored dough into small pieces that they then rolled into balls the size of large marbles. Following Halmunee's guidance, Maya gently pushed into the dough with her thumbs to make a kind of tiny bowl. She then spooned a small amount of filling into the center of the dough bowl, sealed it back up, squeezed the edges, and molded it into the shape of a half-moon.

They continued rolling, filling, and shaping until they used up all the dough. They worked in silence, except for an occasional question from Maya or a low melodic humming from Halmunee.

When they had a tray filled with the stuffed songpyeon, Halmunee prepared the steamer while Maya washed the sticky, dirty pile of pine needles they'd collected from the park. Halmunee took the clean pine needles from Maya and spread a thin layer of them on top of a damp cloth at the bottom of the steamer. Together, she and Maya carefully placed as many songpyeon as would comfortably fit in the steamer before sprinkling another layer of needles on top. The pine smelled so good, and it did the important work of preventing the doughy balls from sticking together.

They cooked the songpyeon in batches until every last one was steamed to perfection. The kitchen filled with the scent of the pine and the unique aroma of the Korean delicacy.

As a last step, Halmunee coated her hands with sesame oil and lightly rubbed them on the songpyeon so that they gleamed as if they were glazed. After she finished, she washed the aromatic oil from her hands and said over her shoulder, "Go ahead. Try it. Eat. You did a good job."

Maya knew they would all taste the same, but she immediately reached for a green songpyeon, from the ones she had made herself. She took pride in those lumpy, imperfectly shaped green half-moons. She had made them with her own hands and they were fantastic. She was so used to the store-bought songpyeon that the softness of the dough surprised her upon her first bite. The sweet filling burst from the center, melding with the subtle flavor imprinted by the pine needles.

The delicious little treats were dangerous. Before Maya knew it, she'd already eaten four of them, while Halmunee slowly nibbled on her first piece.

When Halmunee had finished it and moved on to her next, Maya held her hand out and said, "Let me help this time. We can try out something new. I'll give you my strength and you can guide us."

Surprised, Halmunee stared at Maya before grasping her hand.

It took only a second before they whooshed through time and across the world.

SONGPYEON

By Halmunee, edited with specific measurements by Maya!

~~~~~~~~~~~

Rice flour (1½ cups)

Salt (¼ tsp, plus extra for the filling)

Hot water (¼ cup)

Dried fruit powders or food coloring

Sesame seeds, roasted and ground (3 tbsp)

Honey (1 tbsp)

Pine needles, cleaned

Toasted sesame oil

1. Combine the rice flour, salt, and hot water and mix well until it forms a dough.

2. As it cools, knead the dough.

3. Add dried fruit powders or food coloring to make different-colored dough.

4. Mix together the sesame seeds, honey, and a pinch of salt. Set aside (this is for the filling).

5. Take a small piece of dough and roll it into a ball between your hands. Press your thumb into the dough and make a small bowl. Place a small spoonful of the filling into the bowl and then squeeze the edges together to seal tightly. Roll the ball between your palms to create a nice smooth surface. Pinch the edges to make a half-moon shape.

6. Repeat with the rest of the dough and filling.

7. Boil some water in a steamer and cover the steamer basket with cloth and a layer of fresh, clean pine needles.

8. Arrange the rice cakes in the steamer basket atop the pine needles, careful that they're not touching each other. Cover and steam for 20–30 minutes.

9. Remove from heat and uncover to let them cool.

10. Gently rinse the songpyeon and set aside to dry.

11. Lightly coat your hands with toasted sesame oil, or use a brush, and rub some oil onto the songpyeon.

12. Enjoy and Happy Chuseok!

CHAPTER 23

DAY BEFORE CHUSEOK

Maya and Halmunee stood in a familiar modest and old-fashioned home. Maya studied the wood panels and trim and the minimal furniture that was pushed out along the walls to make room for several low tables that occupied the center of the room. They were back in Halmunee's childhood home. They were in the same room that Halmunee and her mother had been in when they had shared a meal of doenjang jjigae. But this time, they were not alone. Several women and young girls sat on the floor around a table, folding songpyeon after songpyeon and filling up long trays with the colorful treats.

Maya spotted the younger version of Halmunee sitting at one of the nearby tables. Hyun Suk was a little older than Maya, a teenager still growing into her long arms and legs that kept bumping into the people and objects around her. Her sweater was a little too short in the sleeves and her pants were just long enough to pass for cropped pants. Her socks had been darned in several spots, and her toes were threatening to make new holes as they wiggled excitedly against the floor.

"Hyun Suk, stop moving around so much," said one of the older women at a neighboring table. "You're going to knock everything onto the floor." Even though Maya couldn't see her in the crowd of women at first, she immediately recognized the sharp voice of Hyun Suk's mother from the doenjang jjigae trip. Peering around at the other women, Maya found her great-grandmother. Her eyebrows were still as dark and thick as ever, and, just at that moment, were almost meeting in the middle of her brow as she frowned and knit them together. "If you're not going to sit calmly and help, I'll send you off with the little boys and girls to gather pine needles."

Hyun Suk looked up and appeared to be thinking about the options presented to her. She didn't seem to mind the prospect of breaking free and having the opportunity to run outside in the woods. But that hint of disobedience flickered away and she lowered her head and stilled her dancing feet as she sped up her folding of the songpyeon.

"Yes, Omma," she said.

"Don't be so hard on her," said another woman with a laugh, though her eyes were narrowed as though she'd just challenged Hyun Suk's mother to a duel. The woman sat across from Hyun Suk's mother, and the two of them looked as different as night and day. She was dressed in a colorful and short modern dress, and her hair was curled and loosely pulled back. Hyun Suk's mother wore a light blue hanbok, with her long hair, streaked with gray, wound up tightly at the back of her neck. Though everything about her was

167

simple, she exuded a grace and elegance the other woman didn't have. And yet, even with their different trimmings, Maya couldn't help but notice that they were essentially the same underneath. Their faces and hands were so alike. She knew at once that they must be sisters.

The other woman continued, a slight hostility in her voice that must've come from years of practice. "She's just excited about the festival and her new clothes and shoes. And look at those arms and legs. She needs them. She's growing so fast, she's already shooting out of these old, unfashionable clothes. How many times have you had to patch them already?"

Hyun Suk's mother stared coolly at her sister. "Her clothes are perfectly fine. They just need to be let down some more. Not all of us can spend money like water and buy new clothes as frequently as you."

The other woman's face flushed, and before she could respond a young woman by her side cut in to distract and avert a potential fight. She used the respectful term meaning "older sister" and spoke in a calm and pleasant voice. "Eonni, how do you get your song-pyeon so perfectly shaped?" she asked. "I can't seem to get mine to look as good as yours."

Someone else shouted, "If you can't make a good-looking song-pyeon, that means you won't find a good-looking husband or have cute babies! Your husband and babies will have heads as lumpy as your songpyeon." The women laughed and normal chatter resumed, the tension having dissipated.

Maya turned to Halmunee and pointed at the woman who had almost gotten in a fight with her great-grandmother. "Who's that?"

"My imo," said Halmunee. "She's Soon Mi's omma. Soon Mi was my cousin and best friend when I was little. But we got in a big fight and after that things were never the same."

Halmunee appeared to have forgotten that Maya already knew about Soon Mi.

"My imo and omma never got along," continued Halmunee. "Things were already tense between them because my imo was jealous that she didn't have the same abilities my omma had. She and her children couldn't travel back like us. And then the Korean War affected them differently. My omma was always a firm believer in family and frugality. After the war, she always wanted to be prepared for the next crisis. But my imo wanted to forget all about the terrible times and pretend like they never happened. Some sisters are as close as best friends, and others are like oil and water. That was them. Oil and water."

Maya nodded as if she understood, even though she really couldn't. All her life it had been just her and Mom. Although she supposed you could say that she and Mom had been like oil and water lately. She didn't know what it was like to have family beyond the two of them, until Halmunee came to live with them. Mom had been so upset, but Maya had been excited. She loved her mother, but sometimes she yearned for more. And Halmunee gave that to her. And that wasn't even counting the glimpses of an even larger family that she got from these trips to the past.

A movement at one of the tables drew her attention away from her thoughts. Hyun Suk's mother beckoned for Hyun Suk to come and help stack the next batch of songpyeon in the steamers at the other end of the room. Hyun Suk nervously pulled down the sleeves of her sweater and, with her socks shushing against the smooth floor, hurried to join her mother. Maya followed and squatted by her side.

"Today is the day before Chuseok," said Hyun Suk's mother. "Tomorrow will be a time to give thanks and appreciate family. Never forget that."

"Yes, Omma."

"I want you to think about all of that today as we prepare, and tomorrow morning when we honor our ancestors and visit and clean our family's graves. This is our duty. Nothing is as important as family."

"Yes, Omma."

Hyun Suk's mother opened up a nearby chest that stood against the wall and pulled out a package wrapped in thin paper. A new pair of shiny black shoes sat atop it like a cake topper.

"But of course, that doesn't mean we can't enjoy some small luxuries on these special occasions."

Hyun Suk squealed with delight as she grabbed the package and opened it to reveal a beautiful outfit, the fabrics smooth and bright in their newness.

"And we must remember to give thanks and appreciate these as well."

"Yes, Omma," said Hyun Suk. "Thank you!"

"Now, put that away and let's finish this up. We still have a lot of work to do."

Hyun Suk nodded and trotted off to put her new clothes and shoes away. She came running back with her hands empty and her face pink and shiny with excitement. Taking up her station by her mother, she emptied one of the steamers and snuck a fresh songpyeon into her mouth. Her mother had seen, but she smiled instead of chastising her daughter.

"Omma wasn't always so stern and frugal," said Halmunee, just behind Maya. She stepped forward and smiled at the younger versions of herself and her mother, emptying the steamers and eating a few songpyeon between them. "She tried to show us her love the best way she knew how. And so even if she never said it, I knew that at that moment she was saying she loved me. Relationships between daughters and mothers are complicated, but the love is always there."

Maya looked back and forth between Hyun Suk and her mother. Then she took in the groups of women of varying ages, laughing and bickering with each other the way that only close family and friends could. A pang of jealousy shot through Maya so fiercely, she longed to tear through the lonely and empty dimension she stood in and step into the past to join these women for good.

CHAPTER 24

DAY BY DAY

The jealousy Maya felt in that moment never quite went away. Days later, it hung back deep within her, rearing its ugly head at unexpected times and stunning her with a longing that ached in her bones.

Maya tried to keep calm and face each day with a positive outlook, but sometimes it was practically impossible. Her mother was as distant as ever, spending even more hours at her office. It was almost as if she was avoiding home and Maya. Plus Maya wasn't any closer to finding anything more on Dad. Her latest attempt at hotteok had ended in a disaster when she spilled all of the flour and had to chase after and then clean up a flour-coated Gizmo.

And Halmunee's condition was deteriorating. Lost to a different time, she often pushed her own daughter away as a stranger, and kept mixing up Maya and Mom. The more confused she became, the angrier she grew. She kept insisting that there was something she needed to do, but when they asked her about it, she couldn't remember. It would take some time for them to calm Halmunee down and set her to rest in her room.

Then one night, Maya was startled awake by the loud beeps of the smoke detector. She scooped up Gizmo and ran out of her room.

She quickly put Gizmo outside and went into the kitchen, where the smoke detector was beeping. Smoke was shooting up from a smoking pot on the stovetop. Without thinking, Maya turned off the heat, dumped the pot into the sink, and flooded it with cold water, sending steam into the air. Maya coughed as she waved away the smoke and steam. There was a blackened lump in the pot and pieces of rice burnt into the bottom.

"Maya!"

Mom grabbed Maya in her arms and hugged her tightly.

"What happened?"

Maya started to explain but Mom cut her off.

"Your arm! Here, put it under cold water."

Mom held Maya's arm under the running water as a small red welt emerged on her forearm.

Maya said she was okay, but Mom insisted on taking her to the doctor. On the way there, Halmunee tried to explain.

"I was just cooking a nice dinner for us. Samgyetang," said Halmunee.

"Samgyetang?" asked Maya. "What's that?"

"Oh, you'll love it." Halmunee leaned forward so that she was between Mom and Maya. "It's a ginseng chicken soup—"

Mom cut her off. "It doesn't matter what it is. What matters is that you were cooking in the middle of the night and left the pot on the stove while you went back to bed!"

"You always seem so stressed," said Halmunee, patting Mom's

shoulder. Mom cringed away. "I know, why don't we go home and have some dinner. I have some samgyetang simmering on the stove. It takes a long time to cook and should be ready by the time we get there."

Mom let out an exasperated sigh. "You already burned it!"

Halmunee scoffed. "Me? Burn something? No, I never!"

"Never mind." Mom shook her head. "Just forget it."

After that incident, Mom began removing the knobs from the stove before going to sleep. She also made sure to set alarms on the front and back doors of the house and installed one to Halmunee's bedroom door that she'd set each night, to ensure that Halmunee wouldn't get up and wander while everyone else was sleeping.

Just when Maya was convinced things couldn't get any worse, troubles at school popped up again. She was supposed to have finished drafts of the drawings for the school project so that Izzy could piece everything together and make a layout for each magazine page. Maya had only a few of the drawings done, and she knew they weren't her best work.

A few minutes after Maya emailed the drawings to Izzy, Izzy called.

"Are you kidding me?" Izzy shrieked. "This is it? You're the artist, you're the one who volunteered to do the illustrations!"

Maya didn't think it was the right time to point out that she hadn't actually volunteered. Izzy had assigned her to it.

"We have to submit the draft soon to get Ms. Fairley's approval to move to the final stage," said Izzy. "We don't have enough time to fill in the gaps with more articles! And none of us can draw anything more than a freaking stick figure!"

"Stop shouting at me!" Maya yelled back. "I'll get it done."

Maya called Jada afterward and told her what had happened. She had been expecting sympathy, but Jada was quiet.

"Jada?"

"Maya, this is really important."

"I know it is," said Maya. "But I've been dealing with a lot here too."

"I know, Maya," said Jada. "But you can't just bail on us. We need you. I don't want my GPA thrown off because I get a bad grade in history. You promised to get these done by today. The rest of the group shouldn't have to pick up the pieces and carry your weight."

Maya was a little bit stunned. She didn't get the chance to tell Jada about Halmunee's further decline and how Mom was never home anymore. She hadn't even told Jada about the recent samgyetang incident that had made things much worse.

After what happened with the samgyetang, Mom hired a nurse to check in on Halmunee during the day. She was also home a little more often, but on nights when she had to work late, Maya would have to watch over Halmunee. If Halmunee was doing well, Maya would use those nights to cook with her grandmother and bring her back to her favorite old memories that she had shared with Maya. Like hikes Halmunee took with her family on one of Korea's beautiful mountains. Or days when women from the family and neighborhood gathered to make endless amounts of kimchi to be stored in large, dark-brown earthenware pots.

The stronger Maya got at traveling back, the more she hoped that she'd be able to power trips back with Halmunee to memories that involved Dad, or maybe snatch at the few memories of her own from when she was little. She still tried making hotteok every now and then, but for some reason she couldn't nail it. She had tried different recipes but none of them tasted right. None of them brought her any closer to that faint and blurry memory of sitting up high on Dad's shoulders and eating something hot and sweet.

Mom never commented on the multiplying containers in the refrigerator filled with a wide variety of Korean foods, including leftover stews and different pickled or fermented vegetables.

A couple weeks after Halmunee's fire, Maya saw the light on in the kitchen one evening. She peeked around the door and found Mom cutting and peeling persimmons with Gizmo at her feet. The sight of the fruit reminded Maya of the orchard. She slid onto a stool opposite Mom and picked up a piece.

"It's funny because you, me, and Halmunee all really love persimmons," Maya said.

Mom didn't say anything. The only sounds in the kitchen were the juicy whispers of her knife sliding effortlessly through the persimmon.

Maya bit into her persimmon slice and asked, "Did Halmunee used to cut them up like this for you when you were little? You know, with all the persimmons you had from your yard?"

"What do you mean?"

"All the persimmon trees in your yard back in Korea."

Mom paused in her peeling.

"No."

As the knife started up again, the peel of the persimmon in Mom's hand spiraled out like a long curly fry. Maya hadn't tried visiting the orchard on her own yet; Jeff hadn't gotten around to teaching her that before they fought. She worried that she'd never find her way back and that she'd never find Dad's tree.

"Did Dad like persimmons too?" Maya asked.

The knife paused again before resuming its soft whispers.

"He liked them," said Mom.

"What else did he like?"

Mom didn't answer, so Maya offered a suggestion. "Did he like oranges? Because I love them, but you and Halmunee don't really like them. Maybe I get my love for oranges from him?"

"Yes, he loved oranges too," said Mom. "Though they were harder to get in Korea at the time."

"And what about hotteok?" asked Maya. "You mentioned before that he loved those. Do you think you could show me how to make them now?"

"What about school?" asked Mom. "Your big history project?"

Maya sighed. Once again, Mom had managed to find a way out of cooking with her.

"And finals will be coming up soon," continued Mom. "Shouldn't you be spending time on that instead of cooking?"

"Okay." Maya felt defeated. Though she *had* managed to get another tidbit about Dad out of Mom.

Mom cleaned up the peels and washed her hands. "I'm off to my work event. Give Halmunee these persimmons and some tea."

She headed out of the kitchen, paused at the door, and spoke quietly. "It's like I've always said, Maya. Your dad was a good man who left this world too early. That's all you need to know."

After Mom left, Maya sat by herself for several minutes, seething in frustration. Not only did Mom not want to talk about Halmunee or Dad, she seemed to not even want to talk to Maya at all.

Maya waited until she heard the car pull out of the driveway before leaving the kitchen. She carried a tray with the sliced fruit and a hot cup of roasted brown rice green tea up the stairs.

"Halmunee," she whispered as she pushed open her grandmother's door. "Are you awake?"

"Maya?" Halmunee's weak voice cracked at the end. She looked at Maya with a clarity that had been missing earlier that day.

"I brought you some persimmons and tea." Maya carried the tray to Halmunee, who gestured for her to put it on the nightstand. Maya set the tray down and sat on the edge of Halmunee's bed. "How are you?"

Halmunee chuckled. "The older you get, the more people ask that question and expect to hear a bad answer. When you're young, it's just another way of saying hello. Most don't even wait for an answer. But now, there's so much to go wrong with this old body, this old mind." She sighed and smoothed the blanket over her lap. "And now you got more than you expected or probably wanted. Sometimes I can't talk and other times I can't stop talking. I'm sure you don't want to sit here all day and listen to an old woman rattle on. Go, go. I'm sure you have more fun things to do."

"Don't worry about me, Halmunee. I can stay with you. Nothing's more important than family, right?"

Halmunee patted Maya's arm and smiled. "That's right. But that doesn't mean you should ignore the other parts of your life. Don't worry so much about this old lady. I can take care of myself. Now, I'm tired and I need some rest. I won't be much company. You go out and be young for the both of us."

Maya rose and got an extra blanket for Halmunee. Before she left the room, she stopped and stared at her grandmother, sitting up and sipping her tea carefully. Halmunee already looked a million times better than she had earlier in the afternoon.

Maya went downstairs, and it wasn't long before she heard the heavy snores of Halmunee sleeping. She lay down on the sofa next to Gizmo.

"Some exciting life, huh, Gizmo?"

A blinking light on her phone caught her attention. She picked it up and saw that Jada had texted her a few times. Her last text simply said, "I need to see you. NOW."

Maya didn't waste any time responding. She jumped off the sofa and grabbed her keys before running out of the house.

CHAPTER 25

THE REAL PAST

Maya rapped on Jada's window.

"Maya?" Jada pulled open her window. "Took you long enough. Get in."

"What's wrong?" Maya scanned Jada's room, looking for any signs of an emergency or crisis. Jada's room was a mess, but that wasn't anything new. "Is this about the project? Because I told you I'm working on it."

"No," said Jada. "Forget about that for a minute. This is something else." Jada pushed a pile of clothes off her bed so that it fell on top of another pile on the floor. "Sit."

As Maya sat down on the bed, Jada moved her laptop so that the screen faced them both.

"So, don't get mad," Jada said.

Maya didn't know how to react to that. "Okay. Um. Well, maybe don't give me a reason to get mad?"

"I know you said that you never want to see or hear about him again," Jada said. "But after you told me what happened, I couldn't

180

help but look. I've finished the research for our project and was itching for something new. I mean, now I had a full name and location. And you'd mentioned that he'd run a half-marathon."

Maya held up her hands to stop Jada's rambling. "Hold on a second. Who are you talking about?"

"Jeff."

"Jeff? My Jeff? Jeff Chung?"

"Yes."

Maya sighed. "Jada, I already told you. I don't care anymore."

"I know, I know," Jada said, typing furiously. "But I couldn't help it. I had the question and I had the data. You know I can't resist a good puzzle. I wasn't going to tell you about it. I just wanted to find it out to see if I could. But I think you should see this."

Jada angled the laptop so Maya could see. Maya studied the screen and tried to decipher the chart of names and numbers.

"What? What is this?"

"This is a record of results for the Virginia Dogwood Half Marathon." Jada pointed at a row on the screen. "See that row with the blank for finishing time? That entry is for Jeffrey Chung, age twelve."

"Okay," Maya said slowly. "But what's the big deal?"

Jada scrolled up the page. "Look at the date of the race."

Maya read the top of the page several times before it fully sunk in. May 17, 1988.

"I mean, do you see that?" asked Jada, her voice growing shrill as she stabbed at the screen with her finger. "1988! 1988!"

Maya waved Jada's hand away. "Yes, I can read. But this doesn't mean anything. This could be another Jeffrey Chung."

"Well, I did a little more digging," Jada said, taking the laptop back and typing some more. "And you know there weren't that many people his age running the race back then, and the local paper did a story about a group of kids running the race together."

Jada turned the laptop back to Maya. Five boys in matching shirts and ridiculously short shorts grinned at her from the old photo on the screen.

Maya recognized Jeff immediately.

"Is that him?" asked Jada.

Maya nodded. "I don't understand, though," she said. "Jeff knew what time I was from. He knew that I thought he was from the same time. Why did he lie?"

"And you never suspected?" Jada asked. "About him?"

"No, not really. I mean, he liked old-school movies and dressed kind of funny, but I just thought he was a bit of a dork. And when we first met at my grandfather's birthday, he said he was from the same time as me."

"And I thought just the things you did were strange," said Jada. "But this just got so much weirder. You've been talking to someone from the past. Like the real past."

Maya felt anxiety grow in the pit of her stomach. She felt so stupid. Of course Jeff didn't have a relative at that party. He had admitted that he could jump to other people's trees and that they had already met. She was tired of all his tricks and evasion. What was it that connected the two of them? He knew everything about her, and it turned out she knew nothing about him. "I mean, this is so wrong of him to keep this from you," Jada continued. "But it's amazing that this is happening. You've been talking to someone

182

from the past this whole time. That's kind of mind-blowing. Like you could tell him things from the future that haven't happened yet. Isn't that wild?"

Maya rubbed her temples. "Jada, please. Can we just stop for a moment? I'm still processing all this."

"Oh," said Jada. "Of course. Sorry."

"I just can't believe this," said Maya. "How could he keep such a big secret from me?"

Jada nodded. "Yeah. And who knows what else he was hiding from you."

Jada had a point. Jeff could have been lying about anything. The only thing she knew was the truth was what she saw with his tree. And no wonder he kept refusing to give her his number and email address. How could he have kept such a big secret from her all the times they had spent together? How could she trust anything he had told her about himself? About everything?

"So where's Jeff now?" asked Maya. "Maybe I can yell at him in real time."

"Well," said Jada, looking away. "I have some bad news about that."

"Bad news?" asked Maya. "You mean there's something worse than this?"

Jada kept typing. "I think you should see this for yourself."

Finally, with a grim face, Jada gave the laptop to Maya.

Maya scanned the screen.

"I don't get it," she said. "What is this?"

Jada had pulled up an old newspaper article about a plane from Virginia that was headed to Florida and had crashed into the Atlantic Ocean. No survivors were ever found.

Closing her eyes, Maya shut the laptop as the world spun around her.

"Does this mean what I think it means?" she asked.

"Yes," said Jada. "His name is on the list of passengers."

"So, he's . . . he's dead?"

Maya didn't understand. How could this be? How could someone who so irritated her just weeks ago not have actually existed in her world at that time? How could someone who was dead still travel into Maya's memories? Now that she knew he was dead, would she ever see him again? Was it ever really him or was he a ghost?

Maya tried to quiet the million questions running through her mind. She opened her eyes and looked at Jada.

"I'm sorry, My." Jada scooted closer to her and pulled her in for a hug. "I hate having to tell you this, but I thought you should know everything."

Maya nodded. It took a few seconds before she was able to talk. "No, you were right. I mean, I thought I'd never see him again, but because of our fight. Not because I couldn't."

Maya thought of the last words they'd said to each other. She didn't know which was worse—not really knowing anything about her dad or knowing that her last moment with Jeff had been filled with angry words and had ended in a broken friendship.

Suddenly, Maya wanted to be alone. She loved Jada, but she didn't have the energy to talk to anyone, even her best friend. This was all too much.

Maya stood and went to Jada's window. "I should go back," she said. "My mom's at some work thing and I'm supposed to be watching over my grandmother."

Jada followed after her. "Are you okay?"

Maya didn't know. Everything felt numb.

"I just need to sit and think about everything," Maya said. "It's a lot to process."

Jada hugged her again before she climbed out the window.

"Let me know if you want to talk, or if there's anything I can do," Jada said. "Don't worry about the history project. We'll figure something out. Maybe we can have a cookies-and-movies night together this weekend?"

"Yeah, that sounds good."

Maya turned away and ran home.

Fighting back the urge to cry, she tried to push away all the thoughts and images of Jeff that flooded her mind. She kept her gaze on the ground until all that filled her world was the rhythmic pounding of her feet on the concrete sidewalk.

CHAPTER 26

LOST

Still in a daze, Maya slowed to a walk as she turned onto her block. She couldn't stop replaying what she'd just seen with Jada. Time-traveling had been scary at first, but it was an adventure. It became fun. But now she was kind of wishing she'd never even started. Then again, it hadn't really been her choice to start.

Maya was still lost in her thoughts when she returned home, so it took her a few seconds to realize that something was wrong.

A loud sound was blaring through the house, sending Gizmo skittering and yelping from room to room. Maya automatically started to punch in the code to turn off the alarm before realizing she hadn't set it when she left for Jada's. The sound was coming from upstairs. A sinking fear shook Maya's body and made her blood run cold.

"No, no, no, no, no!"

Her heart racing in her chest, Maya ran upstairs, climbing the steps two at a time. Halmunee's bedroom door was wide open, and the extra alarm Mom had installed to stop her nighttime wanderings was blinking and beeping furiously. Maya pressed the button to turn it off and scanned the room. The bed was unmade and the persimmons were still untouched on the nightstand.

Halmunee was gone.

With shaking hands, Maya pulled out her phone and called Halmunee. Five seconds later she heard the ringtone play. Flipping over pillows and pulling down the bedcovers, she found Halmunee's phone.

Halmunee always carried her phone with her. How could she have left it behind? Now how was she going to find her?

Maya ran out of the room and searched the entire house, even looking under beds and inside closets, but she found no sign of Halmunee.

With adrenaline coursing through her, she plopped down on the sofa and put her head in her shaky hands.

What was she going to do? Where could Halmunee be?

Maya debated running through the neighborhood to see if she could find her, but she didn't know how long ago Halmunee had left. She could be anywhere by now. No, she knew what she needed to do first.

Dreading the conversation she was going to have, she called Mom.

"Hello? Maya? What's wrong?" Mom's voice sounded distant. She was probably using the speaker as she drove home.

Maya tried to keep her voice calm and low, but before she knew it the words were tumbling out of her.

"Mom! Halmunee's gone!"

So much for easing into the bad news.

"What?"

"She's gone. I think she left the house. I was at Jada's for just a minute. But she left her phone behind. I don't know where she is. I looked everywhere. I mean, everywhere in the house. I'll go look around the neighborhood now."

Mom cut her off at that point. "No. Stop for a second and calm down. What happened?"

The guilt and fear bubbled up inside Maya and unleashed a flow of tears down her face. "I'm sorry, I'm sorry, I'm sorry. It was only supposed to be for a few minutes. She was fine and I thought she was asleep."

"Stop, Maya. Please, I need to think." Mom's voice was sharp, making Maya flinch away from the phone. It was the voice she used when she was really, really mad. It was exactly how she'd sounded that afternoon when Maya had run away to Jada's treehouse.

"I'm sorry," Maya said weakly.

"Maya, I need you to stay calm. I've only just left the office. I'll be home in thirty minutes."

The phone clicked dead.

Maya sat staring at the phone, stunned. Mom had hung up so abruptly. She didn't know what to do next. Just sitting at home and doing nothing didn't seem helpful.

Finally, Maya decided her next step. With shaky hands she dialed the police, but paused before hitting the call button. It was the first time she had ever done this. But they needed to find Halmunee before she got too far away, or injured. She took a deep breath and continued.

Afterward, not sure what else to do, Maya went through the house again and again, hoping that Halmunee would magically appear. She had never felt more alone. The house had never felt so empty.

Even though Halmunee had been living with them for only about a year, she'd managed to infiltrate every inch of the house and Maya's life. Maya regretted every single time she'd wished for the old days before Halmunee arrived. Now she wanted nothing more than to hear Halmunee shuffling around the house and calling out to Maya for help with something.

Maya also wanted Mom to be home, but at the same time dreaded her arrival. The anger. The yelling. The look of disappointment.

She was so worried, she couldn't even find the energy to think about Jeff. There was only one question that occupied her mind right now—where was Halmunee?

Gizmo's flat face occasionally bumped into the backs of her legs as he followed her from room to room trying to comfort her, until he got too tired and gave up, choosing to curl up in his bed in the living room.

The police arrived before Mom, and their calm demeanor and questions reassured Maya and made her think things might be all right. But then Mom tore into the house, her heels clacking hard against the floor like machine-gun fire. The sound was foreign to Maya, as they never wore their shoes inside the house, and the strangeness of it frightened her even more. If Mom was surprised to see the police, she didn't show it. She calmly turned to the officers with her precise questions and clear answers.

Whenever Maya tried to say something, Mom gave her a look and shook her head. All Maya wanted to do was help, to undo her mistake somehow.

One of the officers stayed with them while others started to search the neighborhood. With the flashing lights from the police cars and the static-filled conversations on the radios, everything felt surreal. Like a nightmare Maya couldn't wake up from.

In the end, it didn't take long for the police to find Halmunee. She was several blocks away, disoriented and dirty. At the sight of Halmunee, all of Maya's built-up emotions exploded and she burst into tears.

Keeping a tight grip on Halmunee's arm, Mom thanked the police officers as she quickly ushered them toward the door.

As soon as the door was shut behind the police, Halmunee shrugged off Mom's hands. Annoyed and frustrated with each other, they both had similar pinched expressions on their faces. But when Halmunee turned and saw Maya, her face broke into a smile.

"Maya, why so sad?" Her face lit up with excitement, Halmunee clapped her hands together. "I know what will cheer you up! I'll take you back to the Chuseok festival. You'll love it. Let's see. What did I eat at that festival?"

Mom glanced at Maya, the crease between her brows deepening. "Not right now," she said to Halmunee. "You need a bath."

"A bath? I had one already today." Halmunee kept her gaze on Maya, as if Maya had been the one to speak, not Mom.

"Halmunee," said Maya, wiping the tears off her face. "Don't you remember? You were lost outside for a long time."

"Lost?" Now Halmunee frowned. "Did you find her? Is she back? Where did she go? Why is she here?"

Maya looked at Mom, but she was busy pushing Halmunee up the stairs.

"Who?" asked Maya.

"Come on," said Mom. "It's late and I'm tired, and you need a bath. Maya, you and I will talk tomorrow."

Mom and Halmunee disappeared into the bathroom, and soon Maya heard the sounds of running water and the squeaks and groans of the bathtub as Halmunee lowered herself into it.

Unsure of what to do with herself, Maya picked up Gizmo and, burying part of her face in his warm, soft fur, made her way up the stairs and crawled with him under the covers of her bed. She kept the lights off so that it would look like she was sleeping, but she was wide awake.

Guilt weighed so heavily on her that she could feel it pressing against her chest. If she hadn't left to go to Jada's house, none of this would have happened. She would have seen or heard Halmunee moving around in the house and could have stopped her before she had a chance to leave. And now, she'd lost Mom's trust and, worst of all, she'd put Halmunee in danger. Maya didn't think she could ever forgive herself.

CHAPTER 27

TASTE OF TTEOKGUK

Lying in her bed, Maya tried to focus on falling asleep. The harder she tried, the more awake she felt.

Finally she gave up and got out of bed. The house was still, with a heavy silence that meant everyone was sleeping. Faint beams of moonlight shone through her windows, lighting her path down the stairs as she made her way around the well-known creaks on the fifth step with the sleepy lump of a dog that was Gizmo.

She didn't know what she was doing. There wasn't anything she could do to undo this horrible day or make things magically better. But a little ice cream never hurt. And she was pretty sure there was still half a pint of chocolate chip ice cream in the back of the freezer. Now that the initial panic that had frozen her with fear had melted into a dull and constant ache of stress and guilt, Maya found that she was ravenous.

As she approached the entrance to the kitchen, she could see that it was aglow with light, and she could smell the aroma of beef and garlic hanging in the air. Cradled in her arms, Gizmo opened his eyes wide and, wiggling his little black nose, took three big sniffs.

Wearing the same apron that Halmunee always used when cooking, Mom stood in front of the stove. Wisps of steam curled around her as she slowly circled a ladle in a large pot.

Maya halted just outside the doorway, surprised to see Mom up in the middle of the night. And in the kitchen of all places. And cooking!

Maya was unsure of what to do next. She could slip back to her room and avoid what would almost certainly be an uncomfortable fight. Of course, that would just be putting off the unavoidable. Sooner or later, they would need to have a talk about what had happened.

As Maya debated what to say, her stomach made an executive decision and grumbled loudly. Mom glanced back over her shoulder. To Maya's surprise, Mom didn't say anything. She simply nodded and gestured for her to enter.

Wordlessly, Maya put Gizmo on the floor and sat on one of the stools next to the counter. Gizmo trotted over and sat by Mom's feet, waiting for a morsel to drop. It felt weird to be sitting in her usual spot, but with Mom cooking at the stove instead of Halmunee.

Now that she was in the center of the kitchen, she saw that Mom was soaking some tteok, flat oval disks of rice cake, in a large bowl, while she heated up the broth she was preparing. Occasionally her ladle skimmed across the top of the broth, collecting the fat and foam that floated to the surface, and then deposited those cloudy remnants into a jar. Maya couldn't remember the last time she'd seen Mom make any Korean food, and she could barely remember the taste of tteokguk, a traditional soup filled with disks of rice cake, egg, beef, and sprinklings of salty toasted seaweed.

The mellow aroma of beef, mixed with the sharp minced garlic in the soup base, made Maya's mouth water. Her stomach growled even louder and hunger pangs made her hug her middle. She didn't know if Mom was waiting for her to speak first, so Maya took a deep breath and struggled to find the right words. "Mom. I'm sorry. I'm sorry about today. I know I shouldn't have left Halmunee alone. I wasn't thinking. I'll watch her so carefully from now on. You can trust me. It won't happen again. I promise."

Mom sighed as she drained the tteok that had been soaking in the bowl and added them to the pot. Still stirring, she finally spoke. "Maya, I know you didn't mean to do any harm. But there's a reason why I tell you to do certain things."

"I know," said Maya. "It was all my fault. I won't let it happen again."

"And what was so important that you had to go to Jada's?" Mom looked back at Maya. "Not only did you disobey me, but you also haven't been telling me the truth."

A small fire flickered within Maya as Mom's last few words sank in. Her eyes stung as she blinked away the rapidly developing tears.

She was being accused of lying, but what about Mom? Mom barely talked to Maya anymore. Mom didn't even talk enough to lie.

"You're right, I haven't been telling you the whole truth," said Maya. "But you're never even home long enough for me to tell you anything! I've been so stressed and busy with school, and I've been trying so hard to watch over Halmunee and keep her happy. It's like

I'm the only grown-up left in this house and I have to take care of everything!"

Mom looked at Maya for a long time. A strong scent of chestnuts mingled in the air with the aromas from the tteokguk. Then, instead of arguing, Mom continued speaking in a calm and steady voice.

"Crack a couple eggs into a small bowl for me."

Maya was stunned. That was it?

She had never talked back to Mom before. She had been taught to always respect her elders, especially her own mother. She wasn't supposed to leave her clothes and stuff strewn around the house for Mom to clean up; she was supposed to pick up after herself and do her own laundry. She wasn't supposed to shout at Mom from across the house; she was supposed to get up and go see what Mom wanted. And she most certainly wasn't supposed to yell at Mom. Yet Mom didn't seem angry. Instead, Mom smiled at Maya.

Maya contemplated asking why they were cooking in the middle of the night, but instead she silently hopped off the stool and got out two eggs from the refrigerator. At the sound of eggs cracking against the edge of the bowl, Gizmo yelped for attention and food. This was their usual routine when Maya helped prepare the eggs for gimbap with Halmunee. But this time was different.

Using a fork, Maya whisked the eggs together until they formed a creamy yellow mixture that Mom poured into the pot. Then she continued stirring in a smooth figure-eight formation. As the eggs hit the hot soup, they curled up, solidifying into long stringy shapes. Mom pulled out a large piece of egg and tossed it into Gizmo's bowl, and he swallowed it up in a nanosecond.

Mom ladled the piping-hot tteokguk into two bowls and set them on the counter. As Maya fetched long-handled spoons and black pepper from the pantry, Mom cut several sheets of roasted gim into short strips.

They had been working together in silence for so long, it walked the border between comfortable and awkward. But at least Maya now had the tteokguk to focus on and to sate her hunger.

After stirring in the gim and a generous dose of pepper, Maya blew on a spoonful of soup to cool it just enough so that it wouldn't burn the roof of her mouth as she slurped it up. She sighed with contentment as the soup slid down her throat. The savory, salty, peppery broth was always the best part of tteokguk. In the next spoonful, she got a perfect balance of gim, a chunk of egg, and several specks of pepper. She next focused on the tteok. They were still white like the rice they were made of, but they had absorbed all of the flavors of the broth so that when she bit into one of them, the same tastes saturated her mouth, but with the unique texture of the firm but tender rice cake.

Maya was so absorbed by the tteokguk, she was almost halfway through it when she realized Mom had set out some banchan. A Korean meal wasn't complete without pungent and spicy kimchi, providing a nice kick to counter the mellow tteokguk. The spicy slices of cucumbers brought a similar heat, but with a nice crunch. Maya also recognized the mild seasoned bean sprouts and sautéed spinach, similar to what she and Halmunee had used in the gimbap. She wondered where all this food had come from. Had Mom gone out to the market? Why?

Tteokguk was such a simple dish, yet the flavors on Maya's

tongue tasted so much more complex than the few ingredients that composed it. Something about it was just so soothing. As the rich flavors of the tteokguk and the spicy tang of the banchan pervaded Maya's senses, she almost forgot about the troubles from earlier that day.

She was almost done when Mom set down her spoon and reached out to squeeze Maya's hand.

"Maya. We haven't talked much lately, and that's my fault. But neither of us has been very truthful with each other, and I think it's time to put an end to that."

Maya looked up at Mom, a question forming on her lips just as a familiar tug pulled her away from the comforting bowl of tteokguk and into a moment from her mother's past.

TTEOKGUK

By Mom, edited with specific measurements by Maya!

~~~~~~~~~~

Sliced rice cake (available at Korean market or homemade; 2–3 cups)

Beef, chopped (2 oz)

Garlic (1 tbsp minced)

Sesame oil (1–2 tbsp)

Onion (1, sliced)

Water (5–6 cups, plus more for soaking rice cake)

Soup soy sauce (gukganjang, 1 tbsp)

Green onions (2–3, sliced)

Salt and black pepper, to taste

Eggs (2)

Small pieces of roasted seaweed (gim, for topping)

Mandu, optional (dumplings)

1. If frozen, soak sliced rice cake in cold water for 30 minutes.

2. Over medium-high heat, stir chopped beef with garlic and sesame oil.

3. Add sliced onion and cook until softened.

4. Pour in 5–6 cups of water and boil to make soup broth.

5. Drain sliced rice cake and add to broth.

6. Add gukganjang and sliced green onions.

7. Cook over medium heat for 20–30 minutes.

8. Taste broth and add salt if needed.

9. Crack eggs into a small bowl and beat. Carefully pour eggs into the pot over the back of a spoon so they dribble in.

10. Serve in individual bowls, topped with sliced roasted seaweed and black pepper to taste.

11. If you want, you can add mandu to soup.

12. Eat right away because the rice cakes will get too swollen and soggy if left uneaten for too long.

CHAPTER 28

NEW YEAR CELEBRATION

Maya didn't even stop to look at when or where they had landed. She just stared at Mom.

"What? How? You knew? You too?"

Mom gazed calmly back at Maya. "Halmunee can do it. Why didn't it ever occur to you that I could too?"

Because Halmunee didn't seem quite with this world. Because she always seemed to have one foot back in the past. Because Halmunee loved Maya and wanted to share things with her. Not like Mom. Mom was too sensible, too rigid, and too distant. She always wanted to act and look forward, only concerned for the future—for herself and for Maya. Not the kind of person to step out of the present reality to live in the memories of family and old friends.

And Halmunee had said it skipped over Mom.

Wait. No. Not quite.

She had said it skipped around in families, but she never specifically said it skipped over Mom.

"Why didn't you tell me, Mom?"

"Why didn't *you* tell *me*, Maya?"

Maya didn't know what to say. There had been so many times she had thought about telling Mom, but it never felt like the right time. Maya assumed that she would know for certain when the right moment would come and she could share her secret with Mom.

Mom looked around and let out a strange laugh.

"I wasn't sure I could still do it. It's been a long time since I've done this. I don't really cook much now, especially not any Korean food."

Realization dawned on Maya as she thought about all the quick and simple meals Mom would throw together. She never stopped to smell or taste what she was making. Was it because Mom didn't want to be tempted to travel back?

"So why now?" asked Maya.

Mom squeezed Maya's hand again.

"There's a lot that I need to tell you," said Mom. "Some of it is difficult to explain. I think I can show you some things to help you understand me better. To help you understand all of this better."

"Like what?"

Mom pointed at something over Maya's shoulder.

"Look. Over there."

Maya turned to look where Mom had gestured. Hyun Suk and Young Soo were walking down the street, holding hands with their daughter, Yoo Jin, between them. They were all dressed in colorful, bright hanboks that peeped out from beneath their coats. Snow drifted from the sky and settled on the tops of their heads and shoulders, which they occasionally shook off. The young version of Mom here looked to be about the same age as she was in the pat-bingsu memory, the first time Maya had traveled back in time.

Yoo Jin's small, gloved hands were wrapped inside her parents' hands, and she tugged at their arms. "Swing me again!"

"No more," said Hyun Suk at the same time Young Soo said, "One last time."

Yoo Jin kicked up her legs eagerly, catching her parents off guard. They all laughed as they swung her back and forth, and she squealed with delight.

Maya gazed at the happy family, thinking about how lucky Yoo Jin was to have both of her parents playing with her in the snow. Maybe Mom and Dad had swung her like this when she was little.

A shriek of laughter behind Maya made her swivel in alarm. It was only then that she noticed the other people on the snowy streets around them. Light flakes of snow fell at a steady rate, gradually blanketing the streets and rooftops in a glittery white powder and muffling the sounds of the city. The scene was quiet, with few cars driving by and stores dark and closed. Groups of children and young couples and families laughed and chatted as they made their way down the streets, holding onto each other for warmth and for balance on the slippery snow. Their hanboks dotted against the snow looked like colorful camellias blooming in the winter.

"It's so beautiful here," said Maya breathlessly. "What's going on? Where is everyone going?"

"It's the new year celebration," said Mom. "This is when all the young people go to their elder relatives' houses to bow, for sebae. From one house to the next. And at each house, you're forced to eat even more tteokguk and other foods until you're so stuffed you can barely breathe. And then you bow and get money. So much fun. Used to be one of my favorite holidays."

The warmth in Maya's belly from the tteokguk she had been eating just seconds earlier was slowly fading away, but Mom's mention of food reminded her of it again.

"Wait," she said, turning around in a full circle, "where's the tteokguk?"

Mom looked at her as if she was crazy. "We didn't eat it while walking outside. How would we even do that? Walking around with big bowls of hot soup?"

"No, that's not what I meant," Maya stammered. "It's just that all my past trips back, it was to the specific moment when the food was being eaten."

Mom nodded. "Yes, that's the easiest to do. But it's possible to extend the trip before and after that moment with enough focus and concentration. And with enough practice, you can do a lot more too."

Maya gazed at Mom as if she was a stranger. She had known that more was possible through what Jeff had told her and shown her. Even so, she couldn't believe that not only could Mom make these trips herself, she also wasn't strictly tied to any time restraints. How many trips back had she taken? How long had she had this ability?

Suddenly, Maya yawned and rubbed her eyes. She hadn't realized how tired she was.

Mom gave Maya a weak smile.

"You know what?" said Mom. "It's been a long night. I know you have a lot of questions and there's still so much more for me to tell you. But I want you to get some sleep first."

"But—"

"It will be better if you're well rested next time," said Mom.

Before Maya could protest, Mom grabbed her hand and pulled her back to the present.

As soon as they returned Mom shooed Maya back to her bedroom.

"We'll talk more in the morning," said Mom. "And we'll go back again. There's something I need to show you."

"What?" Maya couldn't imagine what more she would have to tell her.

But Mom shook her head. "First, get some sleep. You need it. We both need it."

With a sigh, Mom brought their bowls to the sink. But she left them there instead of washing them right away. Maya was surprised. Mom must be really tired.

"Okay," said Maya. "I'll try to get some sleep, but I don't know if it'll be possible."

"A lot has happened today," said Mom. "Your mind and body need the rest even if you don't realize it."

And sure enough, as soon as Maya's head hit the pillow, she fell asleep immediately.

CHAPTER 29

HOTTEOK, FINALLY

Maya woke up early in the morning and bounded down the stairs, hoping Mom was awake too. She couldn't remember the last time she was so excited to hang out with Mom.

Mom was already in the kitchen, and, surprisingly, so was Halmunee, alert and focused as she often was in the morning. No hint of the confused and disoriented version that they had almost lost last night.

"Good morning," said Maya.

Mom and Halmunee both turned back to her.

"Good morning, Maya."

"Morning, Maya."

"Tteokguk again?" Maya asked Mom.

Mom shook her head. "This is something different. I want to take you to a different moment."

Maya looked from Mom to Halmunee.

"And Halmunee knows that you know?" asked Maya tentatively. She didn't want to cause a fight over how Halmunee showed Maya how to time-travel without Mom knowing.

Halmunee laughed. "Oh, I know all right."

"It's okay," Mom said with a smile. And it was a real smile. Not a fake one put on just to avoid an argument.

"Really?" asked Maya.

"Why don't you help me make these hotteok first?" Mom raised her arched eyebrows. "Want to give it a try?"

"Hotteok?" said Maya.

"I know you've been trying to figure out how to make them," said Mom. "Come here. I'll show you."

Mom held up Maya's apron and wrapped it around her.

After Halmunee gathered all of the necessary ingredients, Mom guided Maya through each step. Maya tried hard to remember everything so she could write it in her journal later, but neither Mom nor Halmunee used precise measurements. It was either a spoonful of this or a pinch of that.

"This was Dad's favorite, right?" Maya asked tentatively as they sat down, waiting for the dough to rise.

Mom nodded with a slight smile. "Anytime we passed by a stall making hotteok, he would make us stop and get some. The slightest chill in the air was automatically hotteok weather. He loved getting you one even though I complained it was too big for you."

"I think I kind of remember eating those with him," said Maya.

Mom turned in surprise. "You do?"

"I think so," said Maya. "Nothing specific. Just eating something sweet and hot while it was cold outside."

After a brief pause, Halmunee nudged them. "It's time."

Mom got up, took the dough out of the bowl, and separated it into evenly sized pieces. Mom, Halmunee, and Maya each floured their hands, took one of the pieces, and filled it with a brown sugar and cinnamon mixture in the middle, similar to how Maya and Halmunee had made songpyeon. Anytime Maya got frustrated dealing with the sticky dough, Mom sprinkled more flour on Maya's hands and encouraged her to keep trying.

Mom then heated up oil in a deep pan and placed three of the dough balls in it. They sizzled and crackled for a minute before Mom flipped them over and pressed hard with her spatula until they spread into discs.

Maya picked up a plate for the hotteok, but Mom stopped her.

"Not yet. The filling needs to get nice and hot."

Mom flipped over the hotteok again and covered the pan with a lid as she lowered the heat.

"Are we going back to the same year?" asked Maya.

"The same year, the same day, but a different moment," Mom said in a soft voice. It was almost like all of Mom's sharp edges that had grown over the past year were sanded down.

"Why are we going back to the same day?" asked Maya.

"Because there's more for me to show you then," said Mom. "More for both of us to show you."

Gone was the tension she felt when asking Mom questions. This was a different Mom. This wasn't even like old Mom from before Halmunee came to stay. Mom had never been fully open to her before. But now she and Mom knew each other's secrets. And Maya felt such relief at this, it almost washed away all the drama from last night when Halmunee went missing.

"You're not going to tell me what it is now, are you?" asked Maya.

Mom looked up and smiled at her. "You already know the answer to that."

"You and Halmunee are exactly the same," Maya said with a laugh. "Both of you like to show rather than tell me things."

Mom motioned for Maya to bring the plate to her. She quickly scooped up the three hotteok from the pan and turned off the heat. They waited for a second, thinking it would be enough time for the hotteok to cool down and not burn their fingers. It wasn't, of course.

As Maya bit into the piping-hot hotteok, the sugary mixture oozed out and lightened the bite with a sweet note. This hotteok was perfect. It was nothing like any of Maya's failed attempts.

Just as Maya was about to take a second bite, Mom stopped her.

"Are you ready?"

With a grin, Maya put down her hotteok and reached to the left for Mom's hand and to the right for Halmunee's.

"I'm ready."

"Then let's go."

With a quick tug, they were all brought back to that same snowy first day of the new year.

"Swing me again!"

Recognizing the words and the voice, Maya turned to see young Hyun Suk and Young Soo holding hands with young Yoo Jin in the middle.

"No more," said Hyun Suk at the same time Young Soo said, "One last time."

Maya watched the familiar scene as Hyun Suk and Young Soo

swung Yoo Jin back and forth while she giggled. She turned to Mom and Halmunee and marveled at witnessing a moment from the past with both her mother and grandmother. A moment from both of their pasts. Grandmother, mother, daughter. All together.

The air was filled with laughter and cries of "saehae bok mani badeuseyo" as people wished each other lots of luck in the new year. Snow fell gently from the sky, but not a single flake landed on Maya, Mom, or Halmunee. The snow simply passed through them and piled onto the ground beneath them.

The world felt fresh and alive. As if anything could happen.

"I can see why this is one of your favorite holidays," Maya said to Mom. "It feels so festive and fun!"

"Yes, it used to be," Mom said, so quietly that Maya almost didn't hear her.

"My favorite, too," said Halmunee.

"Hotteok!" cried out Young Soo. "We have to get some!"

"We'll be late," said Hyun Suk.

"It won't take long," said Young Soo. "It'll make the train ride go by quicker."

Hyun Suk nodded and little Yoo Jin jumped up and down, clapping her hands and shouting, "Hotteok! Hotteok!"

Maya smiled as she watched them. So it was one of Mom's favorite foods too.

After paying for their hotteok, Hyun Suk, Young Soo, and Yoo Jin passed by them. Mom pulled Maya forward to follow after them.

"Quick," said Mom. "Let's go."

"Where are we going?" Maya made sure her grip on Halmunee's hand was tight as she flew behind Mom.

"Sometimes the trips between houses were a little farther away than a walk," said Mom. "This next visit was supposed to be a short train ride away. Come along. Quickly."

They followed the happy family on a small road that wound through tall snow-covered hills. There weren't that many people around, so Hyun Suk and Young Soo were swinging Yoo Jin again. Maya loved watching them together. They seemed like the perfect family.

They barely made it to the train station in time and hopped onto the train just before it departed. The car they were in was packed with passengers, all traveling to and from their relatives' homes to celebrate the new year. Maya sucked in a breath before edging between two loud children who were fighting with each other as their mother jabbed a finger against their heads and hissed at them to behave. But Mom and Halmunee just walked through all the people, their steps sure and steady, toward the back of the dingy car.

"Oh, right," said Maya. She often forgot who she was in these trips. She didn't belong in this world; she was just a viewer. She didn't have to push past these people, jostling her way to whatever cramped empty space was available. She could pass right through anyone that was in her way.

But it was still hard to find where Mom and Halmunee had gone in the sea of travelers. Walking through the crowd with her hands outstretched, she waited until she bumped against someone solid.

"Mom? Halmunee?"

"Yes," said Halmunee.

"Stand there," said Mom. "Or you can sit here." Mom gestured to the seat in front of them, where two girls sat.

Maya shuddered at the thought of sitting through people. "No, I'll just stand here with you."

Hyun Suk, Young Soo, and Yoo Jin sat behind the two girls. They didn't say much to each other, but they seemed content, and maybe a little bit tired, as they munched on their hotteok. Hyun Suk held tight to Yoo Jin, who had her face and fingers, sticky from the hotteok, pressed against the smudgy window, calling their attention to anything that interested her outside, which happened about every minute.

It felt strange to Maya to be here with Mom. It had been so long since they'd really spent time together. What was so important about this moment that Mom exposed the truth about herself and brought Maya here? Maya's gaze flickered over to Mom. She was surprised to see that Mom's eyes were closed instead of taking in every second of this moment with her family. She turned to Halmunee, who was gazing at Young Soo with a slight smile.

Maya looked out the window at the snowy landscape and shivered. She didn't know why, but every bump of the train shook through to her bones, and a slight feeling of discomfort and unease settled over her. What had once felt like a wintry adventure now felt cold and empty as the clouds darkened and the wind picked up.

As the train started to swing at a curve in the track, Mom's eyes flew open and she grabbed Maya and hugged her close to her side.

"This is it," Mom said in a strained voice. "We'll be okay. Maya, I love you."

HOTTEOK

By Halmunee, edited with specific measurements by Maya!

~~~~~~~~

Lukewarm water (1 cup)

Instant yeast (2 tsp)

Salt (½ tsp)

White sugar (2 tbsp)

Vegetable oil (1 tbsp, plus more for cooking)

Flour (2 cups, plus more for dusting)

Brown sugar (½ cup packed)

Cinnamon (1 tsp)

Nuts, finely chopped (2 tbsp)

1. Pour the lukewarm water into a large bowl and add the yeast, salt, white sugar, and vegetable oil. Stir until well mixed. Then add flour and stir until well mixed.

2. Cover bowl tightly and set somewhere to rise for about 1 hour. After the hour's up, stir the dough to release the air bubbles.

3. Cover again and let rise for a little longer (10–20 minutes). While the dough is on its second rise, in a small bowl mix together the brown sugar, cinnamon, and finely chopped nuts. Then flour a cutting board or other surface very well. This dough is very sticky, so be generous with the flour!

4. Pour out the dough onto your well-floured surface. Tuck in the edges toward the center and knead it a bit to lightly coat the surface with the flour.

5. Separate the dough into 8 equal pieces and then take one piece of dough, flatten it a bit with your hands, and pour a small amount of the brown sugar/cinnamon mixture in the middle. Curl your hands inward and raise the edges of the dough toward the center, closing the dough up as you pinch and pat down the center part. Do this with each piece of dough and set aside, seam side up. Again, the dough is really sticky so do your best and keep extra flour close by!

6. Heat a large pan over medium heat and pour a little bit of oil into the pan. Place one dough ball into the pan, seam side down, and cook for 30–60 seconds until bottom is brown. Flip over and then gently press down with a spoon to flatten dough into a circle. Cook for an additional minute. Flip the dough again and press down. Lower the heat to low to medium-low and cover. Cook for an additional 1–2 minutes.

7. Remove hotteok from pan and transfer it to a plate. Hotteok is best served piping hot, but watch your fingers!

CHAPTER 30

WHEN ARE WE?

Confused, Maya peeked out the window again. They weren't approaching a station. They weren't even slowing down. If anything, it felt like they were speeding up.

And then it all happened at once. A screech, growing louder. A jerk, more violent than even the one that signaled a new trip to the past. The crunch of metal bending and twisting in unimaginable ways. Terrified screams.

Young Soo shouted for his wife and daughter just as a beam crashed down toward them.

Yoo Jin shrieked, "Appa!"

Hyun Suk clenched her eyes shut and hunched protectively over Yoo Jin, one arm wrapped tight around her and the other outstretched toward Young Soo.

In a blink, they disappeared.

Before Maya could scream, Mom pulled her into her arms, just as Hyun Suk had wrapped herself around Yoo Jin. Instead of being thrown about the train car through the other passengers, her body was tugged in a more familiar motion, a longer fall.

And then, just as suddenly as it began, it ended. Maya and Mom slammed against a grassy bank. The snow was gone, and a brighter sun beat down on them.

"Are you okay?"

Maya shakily lifted up her head, wondering why Mom was asking her that question in Korean, when she realized it wasn't Mom asking the question to her. It was Hyun Suk asking her daughter, who was howling in pain or terror.

"Are you hurt?" Hyun Suk frantically ran her hands along Yoo Jin's arms and legs, checking for any cuts or breaks. Once she was certain her daughter was uninjured, Hyun Suk pulled her into a tight embrace as she quietly sobbed.

"Young Soo!" Hyun Suk screamed as she scanned the area. "Young Soo!"

Still clutching her daughter, Hyun Suk ran up and down the road next to the grassy bank they had landed on, yelling out for her husband.

"No," cried Hyun Suk. "You have to be here! Where are you?"

And then, collapsing in a pitiful heap, she said in a low, crackly voice, "You're not here, are you?"

Hyun Suk hugged Yoo Jin even tighter as they both cried. Their dirty winter clothes and tear-streaked faces looked so out of place among the beautiful green, flowering hills. The same hills that had been covered in snow just a few minutes ago when they had been making their way to the train.

Maya didn't know how long she stood there staring at Hyun Suk and Yoo Jin. Every single thought in her head seemed to vanish. She was in the past and yet she'd never felt so present in a moment. She was no longer sitting alone in a dark movie theater, watching this all unfold. She was a part of the scene. An invisible extra witnessing the main cast act out this terrible moment.

A squeeze on her arm shook her out of her stupor.

Maya looked back at her mother. "Mom? What happened? Where are we? Where's Harabujee?"

Mom didn't say anything, and only shook her head.

"Halmunee?" asked Maya. "What just happened?"

Halmunee looked away, a tear sliding down her cheek. Without a word, she walked some distance away, facing the mountains as if to distance herself from the horrific events they had just witnessed.

"Oh." Maya's hand flew up to her mouth in horror. So that was how Harabujee died.

"But you both said it was a car accident," cried Maya. She turned to Mom. "And you never said anything about you being there too."

"There were a lot of things we didn't share with you," said Mom. "We both had reasons to hide the truth. Especially to you. But this moment, everything you see here, this is the reality. This is the truth. And the truth is that he didn't make it. He got lost in time."

"Lost in time?" asked Maya. "How?"

But before Mom could answer, a car pulled up to where Hyun Suk and Yoo Jin sat, still hugging each other and crying. A door flew open and a young woman rushed out of the car. "Are you okay? Oh!" Her hand went to her mouth in shock. "Was there an accident?"

Maya stared hard at the car, and then at the young woman. She didn't know much about cars, but she knew enough to know that it was a modern car. A model not more than ten years old or so. Definitely not a car from the seventies where they had just been, where she thought they were. And instead of wearing a hanbok like everyone else had just moments before, the woman wore a modern outfit and held a cell phone in her hand.

Maya swiveled back to Mom. "That woman can see them! We're not in the past? I mean, we're not in their past? But where did they travel to? When are we?"

Mom didn't answer. Her eyes flickered from Maya to Hyun Suk and Yoo Jin.

Maya followed Mom's gaze back to them. The shock of the nightmare they'd just lived through was evident in their shaky, stilted movements.

When neither Hyun Suk nor Yoo Jin said anything, the young woman asked tentatively, "Is there someone I should call?"

Hyun Suk slowly focused on the woman and gaped at her, finally taking in the same outfit and cell phone that had surprised Maya. A sharpness crossed across her face and then quickly melted away as she hunched over, cradling her head in her hands.

She groaned and said softly, "We fell down the hill and I think I hit my head on something."

"I'll call for an ambulance," said the woman.

"Yes," said Hyun Suk. "Please go into town and make a call. We'll wait here."

"Oh, there's no need for that," said the woman. "I have my phone." Her fingers flew across the keypad of her phone.

"No!" Hyun Suk quickly sat up.

"But, if you were in an accident, you should see a doctor. I can take you right now. Is your daughter okay?"

Hyun Suk nodded once before wincing and raising her hand back to her head. "Oh, yes, of course. But I just hate hospitals."

The woman frowned. "I really think you need to go to the hospital. There could be something wrong with you or your daughter. They'll be here quickly if I call right now."

Hyun Suk's eyes flitted back and forth between the woman and Yoo Jin as she scrambled for an answer.

"Wait! There's a reason."

"Yes?"

"My brother's a doctor and can take care of us. We just need a ride back to Seoul. Hospitals can be so expensive and scary for my daughter."

Maya couldn't believe how smoothly Hyun Suk lied.

"Of course! I hate hospitals too," said the woman, nodding and smiling warmly. "I wish I had a doctor in the family. Must be very convenient. Come in and I'll take you back to Seoul."

"Thank you," said Hyun Suk. "Let me just calm my daughter first."

The woman nodded and discreetly got back into her car to give Hyun Suk privacy.

Hyun Suk knelt in front of Yoo Jin, still crying in the grass. Hyun Suk's voice had firmed up by now and there was a steely quality to it that had been absent in Maya's prior visits to the past. Hyun Suk sounded more like Mom than Halmunee.

"Come on," Hyun Suk whispered. "We can't sit here like this. Today is the worst day of our lives, but we just have to get through it. And after today, it will be over and we will never have to deal with it again. We will forget everything bad that has happened. I promise it will get better. It has to. Don't worry. Come here."

Yoo Jin held out her arms to Hyun Suk, who picked her up and carried her toward the car.

As she buckled Yoo Jin's seatbelt in the backseat, the woman asked, "Is your daughter okay? She's not hurt too, is she?"

"No, she's fine. Just a little bit in shock."

"Oh, good," said the woman. "I'm glad she wasn't hurt. She's beautiful. What's her name?"

Hyun Suk kissed her daughter on the cheek and then smiled at the woman. "Maya."

CHAPTER 31

JUST NOT MEANT TO BE

Ice shot through Maya's blood, freezing her to the ground. She watched Hyun Suk climb into the back seat of the car next to her daughter.

Her daughter.

Not Yoo Jin. Maya.

She spun toward Mom.

"Maya," said Mom softly. "You don't remember? Any of it? Even now?"

"Remember what?" Maya's voice became shrill. She felt the world slipping out from under her. None of this made any sense. "This is my first time seeing this. Right? Right?"

Mom shook her head. "I thought maybe seeing it would help you remember. But I think the jump forward jarred your memories. You had trouble remembering things for a while after this."

"So that was me?" Maya ran to the highway and pointed at the car that was now a shiny glint disappearing down a hill at the horizon. "And you? And back in the train, that was Dad? My dad? All this time I've been looking for him and I've been watching him this whole time? And now what? Now he's lost? Forever? In time?" Maya stopped.

Dad.

The man she'd thought of as Harabujee for so long was actually her own father. All those times she'd wished she could travel back and see him, she had been. She'd watched him playfully fight over patbingsu with his daughter—with her. She'd watched him at the birthday celebration gazing lovingly at his wife—at Mom. And she'd watched his last moment in this world—with them.

Her breathing grew ragged and a little too fast. She abruptly dropped into her default comfort pose, rocking back and forth with her arms wrapped around her legs. The familiar aroma of roasted chestnuts drifted by. Even though she couldn't see anything with her forehead resting on her knees, she shut her eyes tight, squeezing back any tears.

A gentle touch rested on her back. "Maya. Breathe. Take a deep breath. Everything will be okay."

Maya slowly uncurled and looked up. Mom and Halmunee were gazing down at her, concern etched across both of their faces. Drawing in a deep and shaky breath, Maya rose and stared hard at them. She knew what she wanted. What she needed. What she deserved. From both of them.

"I want you both to tell me everything. No more secrets. No more half-truths. No more pushing me away. I want the whole truth. About everything. The good and the bad. Especially the bad."

Mom gestured for Maya to return to her side. "Okay. Come on. Let's go back home and I'll tell you everything. I promise." She held out her hand for Maya.

And just as she did ten years ago, Maya returned to her mother's arms, and together, with Halmunee, they traveled away from that terrible, desolate spot by the highway.

Back in the kitchen of the present day, Mom cooked up more hotteok from the remaining dough and filling. Maya thought about refusing, as she didn't have much of an appetite at that moment, but she knew that Mom and Halmunee would insist that she eat and not waste any food.

"Every generation or so, someone in our family develops a special power, the ability to travel through time," Mom said as she watched Maya eat. "But, as you know by now, that power has its limitations. No changing the past. No interactions with people. And no travel to the future." Mom paused briefly before saying, "We'll get to that last one later. That one is not so straightforward."

She continued, "There are others like us. It typically runs through families. There was another family my family was close with, but they moved to Busan when I was still young and our families lost touch. I learned everything from my mother. She saw in me the power that ran through our family's blood. My love of food, my sharp sense of taste, and the faint scent of roasted chestnuts that followed me when I was very upset."

"Do I have that?" asked Maya.

"I tried denying it," said Mom. "It was easy since you rarely got really mad growing up. You were so even-tempered and quiet. But I smelled it on you last night when Halmunee disappeared."

"What about the rest of your family?" asked Maya.

"It didn't settle in any of my or my mother's brothers or sisters," said Mom. "They could go with us, but as soon as they let go and lost physical contact with us, poof, they went back home. I was the only one who was able to stay on by myself and make my own trips back."

Maya turned to Halmunee. "Why was it only with Mom?"

Halmunee smiled at Maya and shook her head. "This isn't my time. This isn't my story to tell." She gestured with her spoon toward Mom.

"I loved it," continued Mom. "I felt powerful, special. And I could relive any favorite moment. Who wouldn't love that?"

Maya nodded as she took another bite of hotteok.

"And everything was good," said Mom. "I grew up, met your dad, got married, had you. I was happy. We were happy. And then that New Year's Day, as we were traveling to sebae my aunt and uncle, our train crashed into another. They say that there was an error in the schedule. Two trains too close together on the same track. And those trains were old and couldn't brake quickly enough to stop the collision. Many people on our train died."

Maya's appetite disappeared and she put down her hotteok, unable to finish the last bits. She tried not to think of that terrible moment, but she couldn't help it. The scene played over and over again in her head.

She looked up at Mom, wiping away the tears building up in her eyes, and whispered hoarsely, "But not us."

"No," said Mom. "Not us. Not you and me. And not your dad. They never found him and assumed he had died in the wreckage. But I know I had my hand on him when we left and he was with us, even if it was just for a moment. I didn't even know I could do what I did. But when I heard you cry out, I had only one thought in my head. I needed to keep you safe. I reached out for your dad. I could've sworn I got a good grip on his shoulder. And I wished so hard for us to be safe and out of that train. Anywhere but there. Even the hills we had been walking through just a few minutes earlier. All I could think about was some time in the future when we would all be okay again and this would all be a distant memory. And when I felt us disappear, I was so relieved. I could still save us." Mom's voice cracked. "But you don't know how long I hated myself for not thinking and acting quickly enough to save your dad. I should have grabbed onto both you and your father as soon as I sensed something was wrong. But I didn't act fast enough. I didn't even realize what I'd done at first. It shouldn't have even been possible. I didn't take us back into a memory from the past. I somehow rushed us forward into the future. And along the way, we lost Dad."

"But how?" asked Maya. "And why couldn't we go back again? Why couldn't we return back to the right time?"

Mom shook her head. "This isn't like a quick normal trip back. We were actually, physically in that moment."

Maya recalled the doenjang jjigae trip and the grim reminder of what had happened to that distant cousin.

"We were in the future," said Mom. "The actual future. And we weren't visitors there. No, we were permanent residents. The thing is, we can visit the past but we can't change it because it's already happened. But when you move to the future, that's it. Out of the multiple possible future paths, you've chosen one and that's permanent. I tried traveling back to the past to change things, but it was like my other visits to past moments, invisible and temporary. I couldn't get it to stick. Finally my mother had to stop me. She told me some things are destined to be. And sometimes it's just not meant to be. Like with her lost cousin. Like with your dad. We may have had inyeon and our destinies might have been tied together, but there was nothing I could do to change our fates."

"So then what happened? How did we end up here and not in Seoul?"

"Your dad was nowhere to be found, and we were stranded in a time more than thirty years in the future. All my family and friends were different after so many years. A few members of my family knew about us, but it was kept secret from my friends. They wouldn't understand. They had moved on, thinking that we had all died in the train accident. But I was alive and the memory of all of them and the trauma was still so raw and recent for me. You had nightmares every night until you were too terrified to go to sleep. We needed to make a fresh start—one cut off from bad memories and old pains. So, we left Korea and came to America. I was young and smart, spoke fairly good English, and my mother gave us some money to establish ourselves here. I changed my name and I vowed that you would grow up a normal girl. No fixation on the past. I never wanted to travel back again and I didn't want you to ever learn how to do it. What good would that do? Reliving the past? Even our happy memories would now be painful memories. No. We left that behind us in Korea. You were having trouble remembering things after our jump forward and I never brought it up again . . ."

Mom let out a long sigh. "The problem was I just didn't anticipate Halmunee."

CHAPTER 32

TO REMEMBER

Halmunee.

Maya had almost forgotten about her.

With a gasp Maya turned to Halmunee. She was happily eating the last bits of her tteokguk as if nothing was wrong with this picture.

Maya hadn't stopped to think about it. As soon as they returned from the past, she had immediately settled into her familiar role of daughter and granddaughter.

But that wasn't right. Everything was different now.

Halmunee and Mom had always looked alike. Similarities between them were strong, stronger than usual between a mother and daughter. If Hyun Suk from these visions of the past was actually Mom, then that could mean only one thing.

"She's you," whispered Maya. "You're her."

Mom nodded and whispered, "Yes."

Maya's mind raced to connect the dots. How did someone like the fun and outgoing Hyun Suk of the past turn into the cold and distant Mom of the present, and then end up the kind and playful Halmunee of the future? Maya's thoughts wandered back to that terrible moment in the train and then on the highway.

Of course. That would do it.

"Halmunee." Maya couldn't imagine calling her anything else, even now. "How did you get here? And why did you come back?"

"It was destined to be," said Halmunee as she tucked a loose strand of Maya's hair behind her ear. "It's our inyeon. This is how it happened for me. When I was young I was sitting right there." She pointed at Mom. "So this is how it has to be done. I'm not here to change my past. This is my past."

"What does that mean?" asked Maya.

"In order for things to stay the same, I had to come back here to do what needed to be done," said Halmunee.

"How does that work?" asked Maya.

"Don't worry." Halmunee patted Maya's hand and got up. "You'll understand. It will all make sense in time."

Humming to herself, Halmunee cleared their plates and carried them to the sink.

Maya turned back to Mom. Mom's face was drawn and the crease between her brows grew deeper as she watched Halmunee at the sink.

Maya couldn't imagine how terrible it must be to have to look the future in the face every day, watching it age and slowly unravel before you. Now she understood the underlying hostility that radiated from Mom to Halmunee. Mom hadn't asked to see her future. She had been done with dabbling with different times. And she didn't want to have to take care of her future self as she got older and sick-er. What must it be like to watch yourself decline?

"Oh, Mom. I'm sorry."

Turning away from Halmunee and shaking her head as if to erase the image of her future from her mind, Mom stood up abruptly and wiped the counter with a towel.

"Nothing to be sorry about. Sometimes life just doesn't make sense and can be unfair. Time can be cruel. I thought I had my share of it already, but apparently not. So, no point in moping."

"That's what I keep telling her," Halmunee said over her shoulder as she washed the plates.

Mom rolled her eyes at Halmunee. A gesture a daughter might make at her mother, but they weren't mother and daughter. Not anymore. Not ever.

"I didn't even think about the possibility that she would tell you about the past or teach you how to travel through time," Mom said to Maya. "I assumed that since she was me, we'd have the same interests and priorities."

"We do," Halmunee shouted over her shoulder again. "This is all for the best."

Ignoring Halmunee's interjections, Mom continued. "But, much as I'm not the same woman as that one thirty years ago who knew no great sorrow or disappointment, I'm not the same woman as the one I'll be thirty years from now, apparently."

"Thank goodness for that," said Halmunee with a snort.

With a sigh, Mom joined Halmunee at the sink and gently nudged her back onto a stool. Maya stood between them and took one of the dripping dishes from Mom's hands.

"But, Mom," she said as she dried the dish with a towel, "I'm glad

Halmunee taught me. I'm glad I know. I'm glad to have learned the truth about you and Dad. I wish you had told me earlier, because it always felt like something was missing from my life. But now, in a way, I have Dad back. I know who he is. He's not just an empty hole in my life. I needed to know. To remember."

Mom looked at Maya and smiled. With her soapy hands she pulled Maya into a hug and kissed the top of her head. "You know what? I should have told you everything sooner. I'm glad you know now too."

CHAPTER 33

AN IDEA

After Maya and Mom had finished cleaning up, Mom sent Halmunee and Maya back to bed.

But Maya still had so many questions.

"Mom, what about your family back in Seoul? My real halmunee? Can we go see her?"

Mom continued shooing Maya upstairs. "Yes, we'll go visit. Soon. But first, off to bed for you."

Maya tried to resist, but she found that the trip had drained her more than she thought. Sure enough, she immediately fell asleep again.

Several hours later, still tired and groggy, Maya groaned as the sun shone between the blinds of her bedroom window and woke her up.

It was late, but Mom had said that Maya didn't have to go to school that day, given that they didn't get much sleep the night before and had woken up so early.

Mom had already fed and walked Gizmo for her. Afterward, he

returned to Maya's bed, pawing at her to lift up the blanket, ready to nap the rest of the day away with her. Maya had hoped to get a decent chunk of time to sleep, but now that she was awake, she couldn't fall back asleep.

There was another reason she'd woken up. Memories of the last trip crashed down on her. Her eyes flew open and she sat up.

Mom. Halmunee. Dad. Harabujee.

She was wide awake, but she felt drained from the roller coaster of emotions she'd experienced. She had finally found Dad only to lose him again.

But that didn't have to be the end. She would rediscover him, and she had all the time in the world to do so. She'd never go back to that moment on the train again. Not after what she'd seen. But there were so many other moments in their lives she could go back to. And maybe she'd go back with Mom too. She'd get to know both Mom and Dad again.

After changing out of her pajamas, Maya went downstairs and returned to the kitchen. Mom was there, still in her bathrobe and yawning as she poured herself some coffee.

"How many cups is that now?" asked Maya.

"Don't ask." But Mom said it with a tired smile, so Maya knew that she wasn't being stern about it, much as Halmunee—no, Mom—was during that long ago patbingsu afternoon at the end of summer.

Something tickled at the back of Maya's mind as she watched Mom drink her coffee.

"Mom. How do you know when something's destined to be and when it's open to change? Like with Dad?"

Facing Maya, Mom leaned against the counter.

"That's a good question. And I still don't know the answer. Maybe one day we can go back to Korea and you can ask all your questions to halmunee—your real halmunee. She's very old and weak now, but her knowledge of our abilities is much broader than mine. There's a lot I still don't know. All I do know is that I tried multiple times to save your dad and I never could manage to do it. A couple times I tore through the time barrier, but everyone thought I was a raving lunatic and I was never able to get close enough to warn my past self. I tried everything, but somehow I was always stopped."

Maya knew that there was nothing she could do to change her own past. She couldn't save Dad. Mom had tried. She couldn't stop Mom from jumping forward in time. That had already happened. There was no use trying to save people in the past.

But maybe . . .

What about Jeff?

Was he destined to die?

She didn't know anything about his real life. Yeah, his name was on the list of passengers in that plane crash, but maybe they got it wrong. Maybe he wasn't on that flight. After all, everyone thought that she, Mom, and Dad had died in the train accident but they hadn't. They had survived. She couldn't prevent one crash, but maybe she could prevent another.

Maybe she was meant to save Jeff. She could warn him and prevent him from ever stepping foot on that plane. Maybe his name was on the original passenger list but he never got on. She didn't really know what had happened . . .

She had an idea.

If Halmunee could jump back to the past to do what needed to be done to ensure Mom's future—Halmunee's present—why couldn't Maya do the same? Maybe she was meant all along to jump back to the past and save Jeff. Maybe this was what she should do. What she already did. Halmunee often said that some things were destined to be.

Mom had tried multiple times with Dad. The least she could do for Jeff was try once.

Maya didn't have time to dwell on everything that had happened with Mom in the last trip. She could think more about everything later. Right now, she had to find Jeff.

Maya jumped off of her stool.

"Mom," she said. "I know this sounds crazy, and I'll explain everything later, but right now I need some gimbap!"

Still a little dazed and tired, Mom slowly turned to focus on Maya. "Gimbap?" she echoed.

"I'll tell you about it while we're making it, but I really need some gimbap now. And I think the last batch Halmunee and I made before is all gone. Some bindaetteok or miyeok-guk might work too, but we met more often at the picnic than any of the other places, so I don't know if that makes a difference. And he always said to go to the picnic if I needed to find him."

A week ago, Mom would have demanded a full explanation before taking a single step. But there was something different between them now. The lines that had deepened on Mom's face in the past year with Halmunee living with them smoothed away. She gave one quick nod, put down her coffee mug, and headed straight to the refrigerator.

What had felt like an elaborate and interesting series of steps with Halmunee now felt like a chore as Maya raced to finish. She still loved cooking and she loved gimbap, but right now they stood between her and Jeff and her mission.

As Mom cooked the beef and eggs, Maya sliced the takuan and seasoned the vegetables. And she told Mom everything. About how she'd first met Jeff. The orchard. The things he'd taught her. The secrets he'd kept hidden. And the terrible fate she knew awaited him. And her plan to change everything.

Mom paused in squeezing together the first roll. "Maya, you know you can't change the past. It already happened. If he died back then, there's nothing you can do about it. This isn't like what happened with us. We never died, so there was nothing to change. And you know how I tried with your dad."

Maya shook her head, took the mat and roll from Mom, and finished shaping the gimbap roll. "But you don't know that. You knew you couldn't go to the future, but we did. You knew you couldn't return to the past, but Halmunee, I mean you, did. Maybe we don't know the full story about what happened. There could be other possibilities, other rules, beyond what we know now. Maybe something else happened and we just don't know it. Maybe there's a chance to do something about it. Maybe this is one of those rare instances where I'm meant to do something. Where I'm meant to change things. And I have to at least try."

Maya picked up the large knife at her side and quickly cut through the roll unevenly, the rice sticking to the unoiled knife.

Mom quietly took the knife from Maya and paused. She slowly put down the knife, picked up one of the pieces of gimbap, and held it out to Maya.

"I understand. Go."

Maya jumped to hug her mother.

"Thanks, Mom. Thank you for understanding."

Maya took the piece of gimbap and scrambled to grab her travel bag. She popped the gimbap into her mouth, closed her eyes, and focused hard on Halmunee's picnic and the times she'd met with Jeff there. Then she felt the familiar tug and let herself be pulled back.

CHAPTER 34

JEFF'S PEACH

Opening her eyes, she saw that Mom and the kitchen were gone, having been replaced with the groups of schoolgirls picnicking on the grassy hills in front of the tombs.

Maya raced past the laughter and chatter and rounded the corner, anxiously looking for Jeff.

"Jeff! Where are you? I need you to come here right now!"

There was no answer.

Maya riffled through her sketchbook, looking for the other places they had met. She ran through the trees where she'd seen him on her first trip to the picnic by the tombs. She climbed up the large hill with the stone statues where she'd surprised him with the silly umbrella hat.

"Jeff, this is important! I need to see you! Please!"

Maya continued shouting out at the top of her lungs until her voice grew hoarse. Exhausted, she plopped onto the ground.

Was she too late? Was this a pointless waste of time?

Maya didn't know anything about Jeff's present, the time from which the Jeff she'd come to know existed. What if in his time it was 1990, and after their last visit he boarded that doomed plane to Florida? He didn't know what would happen. She hadn't had the chance to warn him. And now he was dead.

He must be dead, right? If he wasn't here, that meant he wasn't there. He wasn't anywhere.

Maya sat up.

No, that wasn't completely accurate. He had to be somewhere. If not here, in another moment, another time, another dimension.

Maya rose to her feet and closed her eyes. She didn't know what she was doing, but, just as Jeff had once advised, she was following her instincts and hoping that they'd guide her right.

Maya took a deep breath and focused hard on the time orchard. The lumpy ground covered in masses of roots. The simple wooden fence that stretched to infinity. The glowing trees, each standing tall and wide; some simple and straight and others twisted and warped. The dense fog woven through the trees. The midnight sky filled not with stars but with sparkling branches, dancing leaves, and jeweled persimmons.

Her breath slowed. The sounds of the schoolgirls at the picnic faded away.

She concentrated on the first time she'd arrived there. Her tree. Jeff's tree. His brothers. The fight they'd had.

Maya opened her eyes.

Like a camera out of focus, the world before her was fuzzy and blurred. All except for the air in front of her, which shimmered with a sharpness that drew her attention.

Taking a step forward, she moved toward the glistening space ahead of her and whispered, "The orchard." With that first step, Maya fell through the abyss.

What had at first been so terrifying to her was now a welcome achievement. She had done it. She'd made it halfway there on her own. Trying not to get distracted or disoriented, she refocused and said to herself over and over again, "The orchard. The orchard. The orchard."

Finally, after groping the empty area around her, her foot landed on uneven ground. A shiver of excitement ran through her, and she took off running as fast as she could.

As she raced to the gate, she repeated to herself, "Jeff. I need to find Jeff's tree."

She crashed into the gate. It was locked.

Peering through the slats of the gate, she scanned the trees nearby, searching for any with the telltale twisted trunks of those who could travel back.

They all looked the same. Straight and tall.

Maya backed away and then slammed back into the gate. The impact sent a jolt through the wooden bars.

Knocking on the gate, she yelled over the discordant chimes of the vibrations that ran through the wood.

"Let me in! It's Maya! I need your help!"

Maya didn't stop, even as her knuckles grew red and tender from being banged against the gate, until it slowly swung open.

Desperation coursed through Maya's body, making her legs tremble with weakness. She raced through the orchard, searching for a familiar trunk. Occasionally she'd run by a tree with a twisted trunk. But it wasn't Jeff's tree. It twisted too much to the left or the twists were too wide. They weren't right. They weren't his.

Gone was her initial amazement and awe at the beauty of the orchard. The trees blurred past her, as ordinary as any other kinds of trees. Instead of marveling at the thought of all these trees representing countless people, she was dreading the possibility of having to run through an endless orchard. How far could she run? How long could she run? What if she never found Jeff's tree?

Finally, she skidded to a stop in front of a familiar tree. She touched the twisted trunk and a jolt ran through her arm.

But it wasn't Jeff's tree. It was her own.

Maya gazed up. This time, she focused less on the pretty jeweled persimmons and more on the tree itself. The warped trunk, the rough bark, the gnarled branches. Maya had been blinded before by its brightness.

But before she could fall too far into despair, a leaf bounced off her head and into the tree next to hers.

Maya swiveled her head up to the branches of her tree. Then she looked at the trees across from her, their trunks straight and tall. Not a single persimmon swayed from their branches; not a single leaf twirled in the air. The trees were completely immobile.

Maya stared back up at her tree. The branches, the persimmons, the leaves—they were all in constant motion. Frowning, she looked back down at the ground.

The leaves were constantly snapping off and fluttering away, but there wasn't a single one on the ground. Where did they go?

She studied the movement in the branches above her, ignoring the eye-catching persimmons and focusing on the leaves. The leaves weren't falling like they would with a normal tree. Instead, the twigs snapped off and fluttered among the branches until they settled in new spots, nestled against the jeweled persimmons. And some went even farther. Some flew to the neighboring trees, passing other leaves flying across the treetops.

A great number of her leaves flew to the tree next to hers. Maya stared hard at that tree. The way it twisted and then split, as if in a dance. Her gaze traveled up the tree and to the branches, some of which were intertwined with the branches of her own tree.

She'd seen this tree before. She knew this tree!

She leapt forward and touched the trunk of the neighboring tree.

"Jeff?" she whispered. And then louder, "Jeff!"

How did it work?

Maya tried to remember the details of the last visit. She'd been distracted, so busy studying the memories in her persimmons.

She could have been imagining things, or it could have been wishful thinking, but the tree felt familiar. She closed her eyes and pressed the palm of her hand against the trunk. A slight tingle ran up her arm.

"Please," she said. "I need to find Jeff. I need to warn him. I need to save him."

Maya wasn't sure how long she stood there—wishing, hoping, begging—before a faint rustle of leaves stirred above her. She opened her eyes and looked up. One of the branches that was twined around one of hers slowly untangled itself and dipped toward her.

Instead of a persimmon, the fruit that hung before her was a peach. A perfect brilliant peach.

Afraid to let go of the tree, Maya kept her hand resting on the trunk and reached out for the peach with her other hand.

Light beamed out of the peach and smoke whirled inside it. She could barely make out people jumping up and down, cheering as runners sped by.

"Take me there," said Maya.

CHAPTER 35

THE WARNING

Loud cheers and shouts roared in Maya's ears, and a damp and sticky heat pressed down on her.

She stumbled back away from a dense crowd of people, landing on the asphalt. Looking up, she realized that she was in the middle of a race.

Just as Maya stood up, someone barreled into her and they both crashed to the ground. Maya's travel bag flew off her arm and hit the other person in the face.

Rolling over, Maya gasped. She had done it. She wasn't just a visitor, she was actually in the past. She laughed in relief but quickly stopped when she looked up at a familiar face.

Jeff.

Without thinking, she grabbed at the ears sticking out in front of her and turned his face so that it was directly facing her.

"Jeff!"

"Ow, ow, ow! What are you doing? Let go of my ears!"

He took her hands from his ears and leaned back. His mouth

hung open as he stared at her in shock. "Who are you? What are you doing here? If you're not racing, you need to stay back to let the runners through!"

Maya's grin faltered. "You don't know who I am? It's me, Maya."

Jeff squinted at her. "I don't know who you think I am, but I've never met you in my entire life. Now please move out of the way."

"No," said Maya. "I know you. You're Jeff Chung. You can travel back and revisit old memories, like me. We met in one of the memories my halmunee took me back to, my great harabujee's sixtieth birthday party. Actually, it was my mom and my real harabujee, but that's a whole other story."

Jeff frowned. "I understood half of what you said, but the rest about you and your family—I have no clue what you're talking about."

"What year is it?" asked Maya. "I mean, in your time?"

"My time? Uh, 1989."

Maya sat back. Racers streamed past them, but she barely noticed them anymore. That explained it. They hadn't met yet. If the Jeff she'd been meeting with was from 1990, that meant that this Jeff was about a year from meeting her.

Jeff tried standing up, but he fell back down, grimacing in pain.

"What's wrong?" asked Maya

"My knee. I can't stand on it. I think it's busted up."

Maya stared at him as he clutched his leg.

His injury. The person he crashed into.

Covering her mouth with her hands, Maya burst into laughter.

Jeff scowled at her. "What's wrong with you? You think this is funny? I'm injured! I've been training for this race for months!"

"No. No. It's just, this is one of those times! Your knee, your old injury. I caused it! That means that this was supposed to happen. That it already happened. That I made it happen. That it was destined to be. This is inyeon! It's like my halmunee, I mean my mom, said. I'm brushing sleeves with you. This is fate!"

"What?"

Maya stopped and took a deep breath, struggling not to break out into giddy giggles again. "I'm sorry, you probably think I'm crazy. Here, let me help you."

As Maya helped Jeff stand on his good leg she felt a slight tug trying to pull her back to her present. A flash of images from earlier this morning, cooking in the kitchen with Mom, blinded her for a second. She stumbled and they almost fell down again. But after regaining her balance and focus, Maya helped Jeff limp to an empty bench on the side of the street. As soon as they were seated, she forged ahead, doing her best to try to explain what was going on and what he would need to do.

"Look," she said, "A little less than a year from now, you're going to find me at my harabujee's sixtieth birthday party in Seoul. Except the party's not a year from now, it actually happened a long time ago. But we meet when we both travel back to it. It'll be the first time I meet you. You'll annoy me right away, because we both know you like to tease people. But don't worry. You'll grow on me over time."

Jeff tried to interrupt her, but Maya kept going. She didn't know how long she'd last. Already her head was aching from the trip and keeping focused on remaining here with Jeff. Flashes of moments from her present timeline mixed with those of her times with Jeff.

"I don't know how much you know at this point, but you're capable of doing amazing things. Things that may seem impossible to you right now. You'll find others, like us, in the orchard, and you'll be able to travel through different times and dimensions through their trees. And that's how you'll find me. My tree is right next to yours. It's inyeon!"

"What?"

Something tugged at Maya and she grabbed onto Jeff's arms, her fingertips digging into his flesh to anchor herself to him. "And you may think that's all you can do, but it's not," she said quickly. "You can do more than just revisit old memories and cross dimensions. You can also jump to a different time and exist there. I mean really be there. Actual time travel. Permanently. I know because my mom and I did it once. We jumped ahead thirty years into the future."

"Thirty years into the future?" said Jeff. "I don't understand. Why are you telling me all this?"

"You have to remember. Because about a year from now, if you don't remember and you get on that flight and you don't jump out of your time to another, you'll die."

Shocked, Jeff pushed her away. "Uh, I don't know who you are or what you're saying."

Maya struggled to hold onto Jeff. "No! Wait! I'm not done! You have to listen to me! You have to trust me!"

But she was torn away from him and the other runners, pulled back into the orchard, through the trees, and back into her home. She hadn't even had a chance to tell him the details or the date.

"Maya?"

Warm arms embraced her and she leaned into them. She'd tried so hard and yet she hadn't managed to finish giving Jeff the warning. She wasn't sure if he'd even believed her.

"What happened?" asked Mom.

Maya mumbled into Mom's shirt. "He wasn't there. I was too late. And so I made my way to the orchard and I found his tree and I got through to him, or a version of him."

Mom patted Maya's back, but didn't let go.

"It was him from a year before we first met," continued Maya. "But he didn't know me or believe me. As soon as I started to warn him about his future, I was pulled away from him."

Maya jerked back, her hands balling up into fists. "No. I won't stop. I'll try again. I'll find him and I'll keep telling him. I'll tell him exactly the date and the flight number."

Maya grabbed the plate stacked high with gimbap and shoveled one after another in her mouth, her hands now shaking. She was so weak from her earlier efforts, and it took a while before she felt less faint.

"Maya," said Mom gently, "there's a reason why he didn't believe you and you weren't able to tell him everything. Because it's already happened. You can't change the past. It's the same thing that happened with me every time I tried to save your father."

"But what about Halmunee?" protested Maya.

"Yes, but, oh, I don't know, Maya. I don't understand all this. Maybe it's because she didn't come back to change the past. She's just making sure it doesn't change from what she remembered happening."

"Then what's the point of any of this?" Maya's face flushed with anger. "Why do we have this? So that we can look back at old memories and relive them over and over again? That's stupid! It's a waste of time! What good is this if I can't use it to save someone I care about?"

Mom looked at Maya sadly. "It wasn't enough to save the one I cared about either."

Maya was beginning to understand why Mom had walked away from her abilities. It didn't do any good to fixate so much on the past. It was too easy to obsess about past mistakes, to want to live in the past and ignore the present, the lives they should actually be living.

"So that's it then?" asked Maya. "There's nothing I can do to save Jeff?"

Mom shook her head. "I'm sorry, Maya. I don't think there is."

"I hate this!" yelled Maya. "I hate this stupid, useless power of ours. Now I get why you stopped going back. I wish I never had. I never will again!"

And Maya meant it. At that time.

CHAPTER 36

BACK TO NORMAL, KIND OF

Mom and Halmunee gave Maya some room to grieve, showing their love and support in the familiar manner of bringing her plates of sliced persimmons and peeled oranges, then sitting and listening to her.

Then a few days later, after lunch, Mom put a freshly baked coconut cake on the table and started cutting slices for each of them.

"What's the occasion?" asked Maya.

"We're entering a new phase of our lives," said Mom. "There are going to be no more secrets in this family. We all know everything. We all know the truth about the past. And we're going to be completely open with each other. Maya, I want you to feel comfortable talking about Jeff or asking me questions about Dad."

After taking a big bite of her cake, Halmunee leaned back and smiled. "I've been waiting for this moment."

"What moment?" asked Maya.

"This," said Halmunee. "For us to all be one and at peace."

"At peace?" echoed Mom.

"I know things have been confusing," continued Halmunee. "And I know I can be hard on you. But it's hard watching my old self make mistakes. Sometimes I wish I could just shake her and get her to see what is happening. But that's not the way. You need to come to these realizations and decisions on your own."

Mom looked away and nodded.

It was still hard to see how terse and stoic Mom would turn into this looser and emotionally open Halmunee. But Maya thought she was beginning to see the start of the transformation.

"I am too," said Mom. "I mean, I'm sorry too. I know I was cold and difficult. I just didn't want to deal with you. My future. I was hard on you too."

That afternoon ended in hugs and tears. And even though they were all crying, Maya hadn't felt this good in a while.

And things were back to normal, kind of.

With a new determination not to dwell on the past and time travel, Maya tried to distract herself by focusing the illustrations for her school project. Izzy and Emma were still annoyed that Maya had almost caused the group to crash and burn, but they forgave her when they saw how good her illustrations were. Maya's drawing skills had improved even more over the months of traveling and drawing with Halmunee and Jeff.

Lately, Maya hung out with Izzy and Emma more, especially now that Jada was dating Emma. Izzy irritated Maya less now that they were done with their project, and Maya realized that Izzy was a lot more fun outside the stress of school. But even though Maya knew she was still Jada's best friend, sometimes it felt weird having to share her with others.

Maya was so busy with school and her friends, it took a couple weeks before she even thought about going back. Neither Mom nor Halmunee had said anything about traveling back or asked her about Jeff, but they kept a steady supply of gimbap ready in a large plastic food container just in case.

The first time Maya saw it and realized what they were doing, she'd angrily tossed them all into the trash. But the next day the container was restocked with a fresh supply of gimbap. Maya wasn't sure when they made them, as she never saw them do it.

Recently, Mom's interest in cooking had been reawakened. No longer were they eating dinners of pizza or other takeout. Instead, Maya would be lured to the kitchen each evening by the aromas of home-cooked Korean food. One night it was grilled mackerel and a spicy kimchi jjigae. Another night it was jjeonbokjuk, with abalone and shiitake mushrooms simmering in a comforting rice porridge seasoned with sesame oil and salt. It took a few tries for Mom to remember her kalguksu recipe, with noodles so long they could only be eaten if slurped up as noisily as possible. Finally, Halmunee had to help and give hints to Mom on how to make them.

"No, not like that," Halmunee had said. "He likes it with thicker noodles."

It had been one of her dad's favorite foods. Persimmons too.

Maya was happy to see Mom taking joy in cooking again, and she often joined her in the kitchen. Maya had been devastated when she realized she had lost her old notebook during her time travels, but Mom bought her a new one so that Maya could write down all of the recipes she was learning from Mom and Halmunee. Halmunee sometimes joined them, but she was glad to have someone else do the cooking as she got tired and confused more easily now.

Sometimes Jada joined them. Mom had initially been surprised and worried about someone outside of the family knowing their secret. But Jada was practically family, and Mom warmed up to the idea of sharing their powers and enjoying the fun of it. And Jada loved learning more about Korean food and culture with Maya. She was helping Maya put together a cookbook like she had with her own mother's recipes.

Mom wore the same apron Halmunee had used, and there were times when she nudged Maya and said, "Eat, eat," that Maya truly saw the Halmunee in her mom.

Maya loved it.

All except for gimbap. She vowed to never eat a single piece again.

However, her resolve weakened over time, and one day when she was feeling particularly down and lonely she tentatively opened the container Mom had filled with gimbap. The familiar scents that wafted up to her face almost made her break into tears.

"Why not have some?" asked Halmunee as she shuffled into the kitchen.

"I don't want any," said Maya. "I just wanted to see them."

"You know," said Halmunee, "what we can do is special. It's a blessing more than anything else. Don't close up to it like I did. Don't close out a part of who you are."

Maya shook her head. "What's the point? It's not like I can do anything that means anything."

Halmunee wrapped her arm around Maya's shoulders.

"It's hard for us to understand why things happen the way that they do," said Halmunee. "Sometimes things just have to happen at the right moment, the right time. And sometimes we just need to go with our instincts and do what we want to do when we want to do it. It's okay if you want to go back."

Maya wasn't sure what she wanted to do. But before she knew it, she'd eaten three pieces of gimbap.

"I think," she said to Halmunee, "I think I want to go back one last time. To say goodbye."

"I understand," said Halmunee, as she kissed Maya's cheek and let her go.

As Maya's teeth sunk into a fourth piece of gimbap, while the flavors of the seasonings were still fresh on her tongue, she thought back to the first time she'd gone back with Halmunee and all the times she'd met with Jeff.

Maya felt that tug pulling her to the past and let herself slide back. Just this once. She'd revisit the picnic just one last time to say goodbye to the place that originally belonged to neither Maya nor Jeff, but to Halmunee and Mom.

It was nice being back among the schoolgirls, happy to be on a field trip away from the classroom. Even though Maya had seen it all before, she had a new appreciation for this moment, knowing that it was Mom she was watching, not Halmunee. Maybe she'd go back to all the moments she had shared with Halmunee before and see them from a new perspective. Or maybe she would go back with Mom. Get Mom's views on them and gather more facts from Mom's past. From Dad's past.

After watching the younger version of Mom tell the same story to her group of friends that Maya had seen many times before, she wandered off to all the spots she'd been to with Jeff. These were all a part of her memory now. Good and bad.

Finally, she rested on the steps to a small building at the edge of the picnic, watching the younger version of Halmunee—Mom— laughing with her closest friends, unaware of the sorrows that awaited her in the future.

Lost in her thoughts, she was startled when a shadow crossed over her and someone coughed at her side.

"Maya?"

CHAPTER 37

FIVE MINUTES

Maya froze.

She knew that voice. But she didn't dare let herself hope.

Slowly, she turned and looked up at the person standing near her.

The sun shining behind him shaded his face, but Maya would have recognized him just by his ears alone. She jumped up to hug him, then drew back and stumbled over her feet.

Something about him seemed different. His hair was cut short and a pair of dark, thick-framed glasses sat on the bridge of his nose, making him look older and more serious. He was dressed in casual but trendy clothes. He looked like he belonged in the present. Her present.

Maya looked at him, her heart beating faster and faster. This meant that Jeff had listened to her. He'd survived. He'd lived.

And he hadn't come back to her.

Maya had spent the past month trying to keep her emotions bottled up, so when she unleashed them now, anger swept through her so quickly it unsteadied her and she almost lost her balance.

"Oh. Well, I'm glad to see that you're alive. I hope you're having a great life." Maya's voice dripped with sarcasm and hurt.

Biting the inside of her lip to keep from crying, she turned to storm off, but Jeff reached out and grabbed her arm.

"Let go of me," she said, trying to shake him off.

"Just give me five minutes to explain," he said. "Please."

"Fine," she said, turning back to him. "Five minutes. Go."

Jeff sat down on the steps and gestured for her to join him. Maya shook her head and remained standing, her arms folded across her chest. She hadn't fully realized how outdated his old clothes had been until she saw him now, looking like any other boy her age in her time.

"I remembered the first time I met you," Jeff said. "But I thought I was crazy, the way you just blinked out in front of me. Not until I started traveling after Michael died did I figure out what you were. And then we met again. Well, you met me. I knew that I was going to die. But I didn't know when or how, and I couldn't ask you because you didn't know yet and I didn't want to tell you something out of order. So I lied. Each time, I tried telling myself that I was going to stop seeing you. And that it would be easier that way for you when I died." He took a deep breath and shook his head, a small smile on his lips. "But it had already happened. I looked it up and you were right. It was inyeon. We were already friends. We were meant to be friends. We were already in each other's lives and I couldn't stop visiting you. And I guess I already knew I couldn't because you were going to come back to the race to visit me, which meant we had to have gotten close. And a part of me hoped that there was some way you could save me from my future. You seemed to know so much when you crashed into me at the race."

Jeff spoke calmly. For him, all of this had happened a while ago. It wasn't a fresh wound like it was for Maya. She understood how disconcerting it must have been for Mom when she returned to her family and friends and more than thirty years had passed for them since the train accident, but for her it had all happened only a few hours ago.

"I was going to tell you," said Jeff. "But I kept putting it off, waiting for the right moment. And you know what happened then."

Still not making eye contact with him, Maya nodded.

"I almost didn't make it out of that plane. The cabin pressure dropped so quickly I almost lost consciousness. I was doing a trip on my own to visit my brother at his college, so I was by myself and scared. But I knew—I just knew—this was the moment you had warned me about and I had to jump times. I tried not to panic, and I focused all my energy on imagining myself anywhere but inside that plane. I thought I was dead when the shaking of the plane around me stopped. When I opened my eyes I saw that I was back on the ground. And I was alive."

"So why didn't you find me right away?" asked Maya. She tried not to sound hurt, but her voice shook a little and cracked near the end.

"I couldn't. I don't know if it was the shock of almost dying, but I couldn't go back to the orchard for a while. Plus, I had to figure out how to start a new life in this new time."

"But why are you here now? Why didn't you come find me the day I came here looking for you? You didn't show up. You could've explained everything to me then. Do you know how hard it's been for me, thinking that you've been dead this whole time?"

Jeff leaned forward, resting his elbows on his legs and clasping his hands together. "Maya, you're forgetting something important. If it hadn't been for all that, you wouldn't have found the power and strength to make it to the orchard by yourself, locate my tree, and find me back at that race to warn me. It had to happen the way that it did."

"So nothing I do makes a difference?" Maya stamped her foot in anger. "I hate this! We don't have any control over our lives or our futures!"

"Of course we do," Jeff said, as calmly as before. "We do have control, and we do make the decisions that impact our lives. But you're thinking linearly, and that's not how our lives work. You've seen our trees, and you've seen the other trees. That's how everyone else's lives work, but not ours. Sometimes something we choose in the future impacts the paths we take in the past."

Maya couldn't help but smile. "Professor Jeff. Always and forever. But I still don't get what you're saying."

Jeff laughed. "It's hard to explain. Even if the branches and fruits in our tree have been set, they're set based on the decisions that we have made. Decisions we've made in the past, present, and future."

Maya nodded. It was still hard to wrap her mind around everything, especially all the new things she'd learned about in the past few weeks. Dad's true fate, all the secrets between her and Mom, Halmunee's true identity. And the new things that she was capable of accomplishing. Traveling back to her own memories and bringing Jada back with her.

But for now, she wanted to focus on the present. This moment.

"So you survived and jumped out of your time," said Maya. "What year did you land in?"

"I'd jumped thirty years in the future. I kept thinking about you and your warning. You had said that you and your mom had jumped ahead thirty years into the future." Jeff shrugged. "I guess something about thirty years just stuck in my head and pulled me forward. Well, thirty years . . . and you."

Maya quickly did the math in her head. "Thirty years? That's my time, my present! Why didn't you come looking for me? I could have helped you. You just disappeared and I haven't seen or heard from you at all."

Jeff rose and stepped closer to her. "Not yet, I haven't. But I will. You see, I had to find my family first. And whew, was that a strange reunion. I mean they all thought I had died long ago. And they're all way older. It took a long time to explain what happened and show them what I could do."

Maya thought about how hard it must have been for Jeff. And how it must have been even harder for Mom. For Jeff and his family, it was a miracle. For Mom and her family, it had been a miracle, but also a tragedy.

"So they know now?" asked Maya. "You're with them again?"

"Yeah," said Jeff. "It's a bit weird. I had to figure out how to set up a new identity for the present day. Jeff Chung, as I was known in 1990, no longer existed. According to every record on file, I died on that plane. So I had to create a new life for myself. All of my family's friends think that I'm a distant nephew from Korea. Now that everything is all settled I'll come find you."

"When?" Maya whispered.

"Soon."

Maya was sick of vague answers and half-truths. She wanted certainty. Something solid that she could hold onto.

"When?" she repeated.

Jeff smiled at her and said, "Christmas Eve."

CHAPTER 38

CHRISTMAS EVE

Maya had finished all of her homework and cleaned her room. She was trying to keep herself busy so that she wouldn't spend the entire day sitting by the door. But she had no more homework, and her room was spotless.

It was unusually warm that day, and Maya couldn't be happier. This was the perfect weather for her plans.

Jada had swung by earlier to wish her a Merry Christmas Eve and give her a present. "Today's the day," she kept saying. "How excited are you? When do I get to meet him? I can't wait to talk to him. I have a ton of things I want to ask him!"

Jada continued to bombard her with questions about Jeff. Eventually Maya had to shoo her away until the dinner party.

Maya felt like a kid waiting for Santa Claus, but instead of setting out milk and cookies, she'd set out a different kind of plate.

Halmunee was in her room resting and Mom was still at work, though she had promised to come home early in the evening. She wanted to meet Jeff, and they had a lot of prep work for their dinner. They were going to make miyeok-guk and some other favorite dishes.

Maya loved cooking with Mom now. It was their time to unwind and catch up on each other's lives. With their hands busy, their minds were free to roam from topic to topic. And sometimes they just spent the time together not talking, but putting on some music and dancing around the kitchen as they chopped and stirred.

Desperate for something to distract her, Maya gave poor Gizmo a bath. Afterward he sulked as Maya wrapped him up in a big towel to dry. Just as she let Gizmo loose and he raced out of the bathroom, her phone rang.

It wasn't a number she recognized.

"Hello?"

"Hi, I have your journal."

"My journal?" Puzzled, Maya pulled her journal out of her backpack. "I'm sorry, I think you must have the wrong number."

"No, I'm certain this is your journal. It has your phone number in here. You dropped it when you ran into me."

Maya was getting impatient and was tempted to hang up. "Look, I really think you must have the wrong number or the wrong person."

"You dropped it when you ran into me at my race, grabbed me by the ears, and busted up my knee. Thanks a lot for that, by the way."

Maya froze.

"Helloooo? Are you still there? How does this thing wor—"

The call ended just as the doorbell rang.

This was it. He was here.

Her hand on the doorknob, she took a deep breath to steady her nerves. Finally she pulled the door open.

Jeff stood awkwardly with his hands jammed into his pockets and his shoulders up almost to his ears. On his head sat the ridiculous umbrella hat she'd bought a lifetime ago.

"It's about time we met," he said. And then he gave her that goofy grin that was so contagious Maya couldn't stop grinning back.

"You're such a dork," she said with a laugh. "I can't believe you still have it!"

"I don't," he said, taking off the hat and running his fingers through his hair. "I lost it with the jump forward. I bought this one a couple days ago."

It felt weird to see Jeff standing on her front porch, wearing normal clothes.

"How long have you been here?" Maya asked.

"California?"

"No, here. This time."

"Almost a month."

A car that idled on the street honked lightly. Jeff turned and waved at it, and the car slowly drove off.

"That's my dad," he said. "He wants to meet you and your mom when he comes back. My parents are busy unpacking in our new house. He still thinks it's trippy that there are people who can do what I do. Unfortunately, or maybe fortunately, he doesn't have the skill."

"Really? That's unusual. My halmunee, I mean my mom, says it usually runs in families."

"Yeah," said Jeff. "But I guess it's because I'm adopted."

"You are? But you and Michael look so alike."

Jeff laughed. "Yeah. My parents adopted me and Michael from Korea when we were pretty much babies."

"Seoul?" asked Maya. She wondered if Mom and Halmunee might know his original family. They had mentioned there were other families that could do what they did.

"No," said Jeff. "Busan. But this explains why I'm the only one in my family now that can do this."

"My mom's family used to know another family who could time-travel, but they moved to Busan," said Maya. "Maybe there's a connection?"

"That would be so weird if your family knew my birth family," said Jeff. "It would be awesome if I could find them, but for now I'm happy with my family. I got enough going on! Oh, and before I forget, I have something for you."

Jeff held out Maya's old sketchbook to her. "I can finally return this to you."

"My journal," Maya said as she turned it around in her hands. "I thought it was lost forever. You had it all this time? All the times we were meeting? Why didn't you give it to me earlier?"

"Well, I was waiting for the right . . . time. Get it?"

Maya groaned. "Just stop already. You've been here for only a few minutes and you've already made two time jokes."

"I can't help it, they're too easy," Jeff said. "I couldn't return it to you before because it would have raised too many questions. And it was also a very helpful road map for our visits. So I held onto it and used it to find you and all of our visits together. But now that I'm here and I found you again, I thought it was the right time. By the way, I've now found you twice, and you've only found me once. I'm totally winning."

Maya playfully pushed his shoulder. "Yeah, but you only found me after I told you to find me, so I think that one's mine."

"Hmm, I don't know about that."

"Oh, shut up and come in," Maya said. "That's all in the past anyways. What's happened has happened. But now we're in the present. We're finally in the same present. Come on."

Maya pulled him toward the kitchen and picked up the plate of gimbap from the counter.

"I know a perfect place in my backyard where we can have a picnic. A real picnic. I think it's time we stop living in memories and start making our own."

"Sounds good to me." Jeff bent down and picked up Gizmo, who had been sniffing suspiciously at his leg. "Lead the way!"

EPILOGUE

Maya had been spending so much time with Jeff and Jada that she was almost late for Halmunee's departure. Even though Mom offered to let Halmunee stay with them, she declined the invitation.

"When I was you, my future self didn't stay," said Halmunee. "She left at this same time. And now that I'm her, it's my time to leave. Maya has discovered her abilities, learned the truth, and saved Jeff. I've already stayed longer than I really need to. I've enjoyed reliving these memories."

"Are you sure, Halmunee?" asked Maya. Maya continued talking about Halmunee as though she was a person separate from Mom. It helped to give Mom some distance from the bizarre situation of talking about her future self.

"Yes," said Halmunee. She looked at Mom and smiled. "People shouldn't have to be with their future selves. It's too eerie. I came here just as I remembered from my past to help Maya, and to help get rid of the secrets between you two, and I've done that. I have my own life waiting for me in my time. And I need to go back before it gets too hard for me to remember my present. It's a struggle staying here. Time jumps back can muddle up the mind if you stay too long."

Mom looked up sharply at Halmunee. "What? What did you say?"

"Huh?"

"What did you say just now?"

Halmunee frowned as she tried to remember.

"About time jumps messing with your mind if you stay too long," said Mom. "Is that what's causing your memory loss? It's not dementia?"

Realization spread across Halmunee's face.

"Ah," she said. "That's what you were so worried about. Yes, staying too long in the past can cause memory issues. Going forward you've chosen the future path and that's permanent. But trying to go back to the past is harder in a lot of ways. Not only is it impossible if it's not destined to be, but the times you can go back require constant concentration to hold onto that timeline. It gets confusing. Humans weren't meant to keep more than one timeline in their minds for too long."

Maya remembered how hard it had been to travel back to the past, to Jeff's race, and stay there long enough to give the warning. She couldn't imagine doing it for several months.

"Is it permanent?" asked Mom.

Halmunee laughed and shook her head. "No, I'll be back to normal once I get back and get some rest. No time jumping for me for a while."

Keeping track of the timelines and rules was so confusing. What was supposed to happen? What had already happened?

Mom jumped up and squeezed Halmunee in a tight embrace.

"Thank you," said Mom. "Thank you."

"I'm sorry, I thought I told you," said Halmunee. "I have trouble keeping track of what I've said or haven't said here."

Mom laughed as she nodded and wiped away tears that spilled down her face.

"Well, I know now," she said. "And I'm sure you know how relieved I am. Not just for me, but for Maya too."

Both Mom and Halmunee turned to Maya and smiled at her. Two similar faces, separated only by time.

"Oh, I'm glad I remembered this before I left," said Halmunee. "But now it's really time for me to go."

"Well then, what do we need to cook?" Maya gestured to the kitchen.

"Nothing," said Halmunee. "I've been concentrating and focusing on staying in this time. It hasn't been easy. All I need to do is let go and I'll get pulled back to my own time. I can finally relax."

Halmunee patted Mom's arm. "Thank you for everything. I know it wasn't easy."

Mom nodded.

Halmunee turned to Maya. "Now, come here and let me say goodbye to you."

A wave of panic washed over Maya. "I'm still there in your time, aren't I? Why are you acting like this is the last time you'll see me?"

Halmunee looked at her confused. "What do you mean? Of course you're still in my time. Now come here. I want to give my granddaughter a hug."

Mom and Maya exchanged a look. Did Halmunee really forget that Maya was her daughter and not her granddaughter? Or was she just so used to calling Maya her granddaughter that she got a little confused? Either way, Halmunee needed to get back while she was still having a good and lucid morning.

Maya gave Halmunee a big hug and whispered in her ear, "Goodbye, Halmunee. Mom. I'll miss you so much here, but I'm happy you'll be back home in your right time."

"Don't let me grow distant from you again," said Halmunee. "I just needed a little bit of a nudge from my future self. Now that I've come back and shown you everything, there are no more secrets in this family. Nothing to stand between the two of you. And maybe one day you'll be able to search all of time and find those who are lost. Maybe you already have."

Halmunee kissed Maya on the cheek and stepped back.

"Besides, it's time to return to my own family, in my time. We've spent too much time apart. Our inyeon is pulling me back. He's waiting for me."

Before Maya could ask what she meant, Halmunee disappeared one last time.

ACKNOWLEDGMENTS

None of this would have been possible without the love, support, and food of my family. Thank you to my mom, Young Suk Ahn, who always fed me well during our weekend lunches, and to my dad, Byung Cho Ahn, who frequently retold his favorite childhood stories to me. I remember fondly our lunch over doenjang jjigae and mackerel when I pestered you both with my questions about food from your past. Mom, thank you for your recipe advice and making sure that my depictions of your past were accurate. I only wish that Dad could have seen my book be published. Thank you to my niblings, Kyungsup Hwang and Theodore Hwang, who were my first readers. I started writing children's books because of you. My writing kept pace with you as you grew up, and I hope that you never outgrow my books no matter how old you get. Thank you to my oldest sister and brother-in-law, Cathy Ahn and Adon Hwang; thank you for looking out for me and for raising such amazing kids. I can't even count the number of Sunday meals you hosted and all of the advice you've given me. And thank you to my middle sister, Jenny Ahn, for always managing to make me laugh when I'm down and letting me know that it's okay to be weird. You were and continue to be one of the biggest influences in my life.

Then there are all of my friends, who were always there to answer my questions and celebrate with me. Thank you to Morgan Burrell (mfr), who is essentially my life coach and was an early reader back when this book had a different title. You're my Jada, even though you're actually totally not like Jada. Thank you to Dafina Stewart and Keisha

Patrick, my pod buddies who kept me company throughout this process with our group chat. And to Andrea Lucan, who encouraged me to keep this book as true to my Asian American identity as possible. I'd like to thank the rest of my friends who provided support in all different ways, but especially Steven Lauridsen, Michelle Kidd, Patricia Yeh, and Adam Cohen and his wonderful daughter, Juliet.

This story wouldn't have become the book that you hold in your hands if it weren't for the amazing team behind it. Thank you to my agent, Melissa Edwards, who never gave up on me and this story. You've been my biggest advocate and protector, steering me through the strange waters of the publication world. Thank you to my editor, Alex Arnold, who saw a future for this book that went beyond my dreams and pushed me to make this a better story. And thank you to Jessica Yang for your input and understanding of what it's like to be raised as an Asian American. To the rest of the Quirk team who all played a part in putting this book together and getting it across the finish line, thank you so much. You gave everything I could have possibly hoped for with this book. And thank you to Jenny Park for her beautiful illustrations that perfectly captured the images in my head.

Then there are those I don't have room to name, including all the listeners of *The Golden Orchard*, readers of my Pug Pals books, and friends and followers on social media. Thank you for giving your love to my earlier works and random posts.

And I couldn't leave out my pugs, Sunny, Rosy, Monkey, and Pika, who provided the same love and support that Gizmo provided Maya.

Finally, thanks to you, for reading my book to the very end.